"I should never have come here...

"I came for all the wrong reasons." Suddenly a flood of words gushed out of Dana. "It's your land, it's your family, this is your town and I just came here and…"

Mason pulled back. "And changed *everything*."

"For the worse," she insisted.

"Feels like it at the moment." He smoothed back a lock of her hair. "But I'm not sorry."

"How can you say that? The things people said…" They'd stopped just short of accusing him of selling out the town to a shady cause in order to save his own skin. Someone had even used the word *contaminate*. How could he look at some of these people as neighbors ever again?

"I'm not sorry," he repeated. "It's not turned out anything close to how I wanted. How I expected, even. But I can't say I'm sorry that you're…here. That you're in my life. In Charlie's life."

Mason held her gaze…and Dana's legs felt unsteady beneath her for a whole different reason.

Allie Pleiter, an award-winning author and RITA® Award finalist, writes both fiction and nonfiction. Her passion for knitting shows up in many of her books and all over her life. Entirely too fond of French macarons and lemon meringue pie, Allie spends her days writing books and avoiding housework. Allie grew up in Connecticut, holds a BS in speech from Northwestern University and lives near Chicago, Illinois.

Books by Allie Pleiter

Love Inspired

Wander Canyon

Their Wander Canyon Wish
Winning Back Her Heart
His Christmas Wish
A Mother's Strength
Secrets of Their Past
A Place to Heal

Matrimony Valley

His Surprise Son
Snowbound with the Best Man
Wander Canyon Courtship

Visit the Author Profile page at LoveInspired.com for more titles.

A Place to Heal

Allie Pleiter

LOVE INSPIRED
INSPIRATIONAL ROMANCE

LOVE INSPIRED®
INSPIRATIONAL ROMANCE

ISBN-13: 978-1-335-58509-7

A Place to Heal

Copyright © 2022 by Alyse Stanko Pleiter

For questions and comments about the quality of this book, please contact us
at CustomerService@Harlequin.com.

Love Inspired
22 Adelaide St. West, 41st Floor
Toronto, Ontario M5H 4E3, Canada
www.LoveInspired.com

Printed in U.S.A.

Thou, which hast shewed me great and sore troubles, shalt quicken me again, and shalt bring me up again from the depths of the earth.
—*Psalm* 71:20

To Pastor Lauren

One of my favorite recent new beginnings

Chapter One

Dana Preston fought the dry Arizona wind as she spread the map out on the hood of her car. She compared the bright red circle on her map to the address on the gate across the road in front of her. "Yep," she declared to the April sky and the dusty roadside, "this is the place."

Even though she did not grow up in North Springs—her childhood home was closer to Phoenix—it felt familiar. The sense of space here was so strong you could feel it. Almost touch it, like a cold Denver snowfall or a thick fog. It was a different kind of mountain air, yes, but the clarity and the wide-openness of it made her feel *human* again. Significant, but not the life-and-death stakes she'd just made the choice to leave. Different. Possible, if that made any sort of sense. It had been a while since Dana felt a surge of any kind of hope.

Which was good. Hope was why she was here.

She'd never been the dream-chaser type, but then again she'd not ever been shot in the abdomen before, either. She was different now, and her old life in Denver just didn't fit anymore. All she knew was that she had to come here and had to try. She had no idea if this life would fit. It was *entirely possible* she was looking at an impractical pipe dream.

If she were honest, it was likely. No one in Denver would ever believe she was toying with the ideas that filled the file folder on her passenger seat. Dana climbed to sit on the hood of her car, wincing as she did. It bugged her that the surgery wounds still hurt. They would bother her for another six months, the doctor had said. "Not all the time, just when you ask the wrong thing of those muscles."

"That's enough of that," she lectured her abdominal wall, shifting further onto the hood despite the jolt of pain radiating out of the scar that ran across her belly below her navel. The zing of pain stopped as she settled herself next to the map. She needed to think, and she wanted to do that staring at the thing she was thinking about: the camp.

Of course, she wasn't staring at a camp. She was staring at the run-down front gate of Mason Avery's property. The chain-link gate was old and creaky-looking. A battered No Trespassing sign hung off one of its fasteners in the opposite of a welcome. It squeaked and clanged a warning as it swung in the same wind that kept trying to steal her map off the hood of the car.

Fencing on either side of the gate stretched far in both directions. She'd done her homework; the property was a full twenty acres. Good land, right size, a perfect creek and mountain spring running right through it, old enough to be affordable but not too run-down.

At least she hoped not too run-down. The sizable plot of mountainside land had everything she was looking for—except a willing seller.

In fact, the property in front of her wasn't even up for sale. *Yet.* All the properties that *were* on the market loomed beyond her means at the moment, so she'd had to get creative. Find the right land first, then convince the owner to sell it to her. *Not exactly the way people do this*, she told herself. Then again, what sort of people did *this*? At every stage of this irrational journey, half of her kept hoping things would fall through. That life would hand her an excuse *not* to do this.

In fact, just the opposite had happened. She'd been able to extend her medical leave indefinitely, pack up and leave Denver, work out sufficient finances, make the trip here, and find a nice place to stay. Dana didn't know what to make of the fact that all her obstacles kept disappearing.

And now here she was, staring at a gate, contemplating how to turn the land behind it into a camp for kids who had lost a parent to violence or trauma. *Practical people like you don't do things like this. Don't even consider doing things like this.* And yet the idea had taken hold of her in the days after the shooting and the surgery, and had not let go since.

How? Why? When—now? Someday? Never? Dana chose to just sit with the avalanche of doubts, to perch on the hood of her car with the acres in view and see if the mountains or the sky or the steady spring wind would give up any secrets to help her.

She'd been there perhaps twenty minutes when a

squeaky noise caught her attention. A young boy—about seven or eight by the looks of it—rode up the gravel drive on a bicycle. *Charlie.* Mason's young son.

Dana watched him approach, keen to all the signals kids gave off. Years as a detective specializing in juvenile violence gave her a radar for that sort of thing. Charlie was wary, but curious. A bit defiant and defensive, as if bravery came easy when the gate was locked.

Dana didn't get the sense that the gate was opened often. It was two o'clock on a Tuesday—why wasn't Charlie in school?

He rode his bike right up to the gate, the chain-link rattling when his front tire bumped up against it. It sent the No Trespassing sign swinging again. His oddly steady stare unnerved Dana—and not many things unnerved her after all the ugliness and violence she'd witnessed.

"Hello," she called from her side of the road. It seemed like the thing to say.

Charlie stood there, still astride his bicycle, staring at her. He stuffed his hands in his pockets and chewed something—gum? his lip?—as he leveled her with a narrow-eyed glare way too old for his tender years. One foot tapped against the ground as if he couldn't quite pull off the steely stance he was trying to show her.

It seemed ridiculous to try "Hello" again, so she folded the map and gingerly slid off the hood of the car. She leaned against the fender and mirrored Charlie's stance by putting both her hands in the pockets of her jeans.

"Who're you?" he asked after a solid minute of stare-down.

Funny how the simple questions can be the hardest to

answer. *I used to be a police detective, but now I don't think I am anymore because I got shot and I don't want to go back* was probably a longer answer than what the kid was looking for. She settled for "I'm Dana."

Charlie bumped his bike up against the gate again, maybe to remind her it was there between them. "Dana who?"

"Dana Preston." This was the first time in a long time she didn't preface those two words with "Detective." Technically, she was still a detective. She'd gotten her six-month leave reclassified as "indefinite," but she knew it was permanent. Dana wasn't here to buy a vacation home. She was here to either launch a totally new life or get a wild dream out of her system.

"Why're you staring at me?"

Dana took a small step toward Charlie. "I'm not staring at you."

His chin rose and one hand came out of its pocket. "Yeah, you are."

Dana took another step toward Charlie and let one of her own hands come out from a pocket. "No, I'm looking at the land around you. Why are you staring at me?"

"Am not," Charlie countered. He scuffed the gravel with the foot that had been tapping. "Are you looking at Grandpa's house?"

So it *was* family land. She'd gone back through the county records to see that the land had originally been purchased by Dwight Avery, Mason's father. He'd been prosperous in his day, but Mason wasn't. Barely scraping by, from the looks of it. Dana needed a motivated seller, one that might like very much to stay on the property and help with the upkeep. Mason fit that bill—she hoped. "Sort of," she replied, reminding herself to keep the law enforcement edge out of her voice. "I'm looking at all of it, actually."

"Why?" Charlie's free hand rose to the handlebar of his bicycle, signaling that he could turn around and ride right out of there if he didn't like the answer she gave.

Dana opted for something close to the truth. "Not sure yet, actually. I probably need to ask your dad, I suppose."

Charlie's eyes widened. "How do you know I've got a dad?"

Dana risked another step—which put her out into the road, so she kept one ear cocked for the sound of a car coming around the mountain road's many bends. "Everybody's got a dad. Just a question of whether or not they're around. Or nice," she added, remembering the last gut-wrenching abuse case she'd worked back in Denver. "Nice" most definitely did not apply. She had made sure "criminal endangerment" did.

"Mine's here." His chin rose slightly as he said that, as if it was something that needed defending.

"Is he nice?" It probably was a risk to ask, but Dana couldn't help herself. Charlie's answer might tell her a lot about who she'd be dealing with. Intel was never a bad thing, even when chasing outrageous dreams.

"He's *Dad.*" A shrug and an eye roll accompanied the declaration. That could have meant anything from *dads are never nice and sometimes they hit* to *he won't let me eat ice cream for breakfast.*

It struck her, watching the way Charlie stared at her with narrow eyes, that the boy looked too old for his body.

Scruffy hair and gangly limbs but a straight spine. A little lost with a hard edge that didn't belong on someone that small. As if someone had managed to stuff a thirteen-year-old inside his skin when no one was looking.

Maybe no one *was* looking. After all, the kid couldn't have been more than seven or eight and he was wandering around near the road with no adult in sight on what should have been a school day.

Dana felt that tug, that relentless obligation that made the fellow officers in her old precinct nickname her "Mom." The sense of duty that made her very good at her job.

And very nearly gotten her killed.

Mason Avery looked up from the workbench and felt his whole body slump. Charlie was gone. "Charlie? Charlie!"

His son was so good at disappearing the kid should pursue a career in espionage. Seven-year-olds should be cute and charming, not wily and exasperating. "Charlie!" he called again, dashing through the rooms of the large house in search of the boy. *I should never have believed the bit about the stomachache. I should have insisted he go to school.*

It was never a good thing to feel outsmarted by your own second grader, and Mason felt as if that was happening far too often lately. *Our boy...* Mason moaned to the memory of his late wife as he took the stairs two at a time up to Charlie's bedroom. *You were always so much better at this than me.*

The huge property was securely fenced—and gated—

but none of that replaced the constant supervision Charlie ought to have. Gone to the kitchen for a juice box was not the same as vanishing from sight while Mason looked down for half a minute to finish fitting a dovetail drawer joint.

Mason turned in desperate circles about the room, hands fisted in his unruly hair, looking for clues to where Charlie had taken off to now. *Melony, I'm failing him. This is so hard.*

Out the window, he spotted Charlie. He was far down the drive, all the way to the gate. And he was talking to someone.

Mason took the stairs three at a time down toward the front door and sprinted down the gravel after his son. The gate was always locked, but that didn't stop the surge of panic that sped Mason's steps. Charlie was developing a worrying talent for getting into things that weren't good for him, and the woman on the other side of the fence didn't look at all familiar. School official? Child services? Another annoying land developer looking to turn his land into a subdivision?

"Charlie!" he yelled when he was still a ways away, hoping his son would turn around and come to him. He didn't. More often than not these days, he didn't. It was like Charlie was slipping down the mountain slope away from him, and all the prayer and care Mason could douse on him did little to stop the landslide.

Don't yell, he lectured himself, slowing his steps and tamping down his frustration as he neared Charlie and the visitor on the other side of the gate. "Hey, buddy, you're supposed to be on the couch in my workshop reading. Whatcha doing all the way out here?"

Charlie turned with an "Oh, hi" expression as if house escapes on supposed sick days were perfectly okay. "Talking to her."

Mason was relieved "her"—whoever she was—was neither in a developer's slick suit or a uniform. Still, that was little comfort. "And who are you?" It would have been smarter not to make that so much of an accusation, but Mason's last bastion of good manners had been stomped out weeks ago.

"Dana Preston."

Mason didn't know what to make of the fact that no title came with the name. She didn't say "officer" or "from the county." Tall and fit with an efficient bob of blond hair, she was head-turning, but not in a "knockout beauty" kind of way. Her stance and the power in her eyes—even from here—demanded notice. She looked close to his age, which was a welcome change from the battalion of well-intentioned church aunties who occasionally forced visits on him. Those women always called first, and often brought cookies and casseroles to soften their list of concerned questions.

He walked closer to the gate. "Can I help you?" He was proud of choosing that over "What are you doing staring through my fence talking to my son?" But he still put a protective hand on Charlie's shoulder—at least until Charlie shrugged it off with a "Daaaaaad" worthy of a grumpy teen.

"You own this place?" Ms. Preston cast her glance around as if she knew just how far the land and the fence extended.

Eyeing the land. The moment of him finding her nice-looking evaporated like a puddle in August. *One of those.*

Mason was trying hard to hold on to the family land for Charlie's sake, and it didn't help that greedy developers kept knocking on his door. No stack of bills would ever be high enough to make him sell this place to become vacation condos. Ever.

Mason met her eyes with all the welcome of the well-locked gate. "I'm not selling."

She must have worked hard to master that look of surprise. "How do you know I'm looking to buy?"

"You all are," he shot back. "Nice touch trying to get at me through my son, by the way. Really adds to the charm."

"He rode up to me and asked first, not that I'm sure it would make any difference to you."

That wasn't welcome news. Mason looked down at Charlie for an explanation.

"She started it," Charlie whined. "She was just sitting there on her car staring at us."

One corner of Ms. Preston's mouth turned up at that. "I suppose I did start it. I was sitting on my car consulting my map and my notes and looking at your property. But I did not lure your son to the gate, if that's what you're thinking."

Mason pointed at her. "So you *are* looking to buy."

She shifted her weight. At least she had the decency to realize she hadn't made the best first impression. "I'd like to talk to you about it, yes." Mason waited for her to push a business card through the chain link of the fence. Three others had tried that, and their cards were still lying somewhere in the grass.

"Save your breath, Ms. Preston. I'm not interested."

He was about to grab the handlebars of Charlie's bike and lead them both back to the house when she cut in. "I'd really like the chance to tell you what I have in mind. It's not what you think."

She could paint a picture of the world's most luxurious dwellings and tout a mile-high stack of money for all he cared. It wouldn't make a bit of difference. He turned Charlie's bike around and started walking. "I'm not selling," he called back over his shoulder without looking.

He heard the chain link rattle as she must have put her hands on the gate. He'd give her points for sheer persistence and guts. "I want to build a camp for kids. Ones who have lost a parent to violence," she shouted to his turned back.

Mason's steps halted even as he told himself to keep walking. Charlie's eyes widened, and his son looked up with an expression that knocked the breath from Mason's lungs. "You mean kids like me?"

Mason tightened his grip on the handlebar, counted to five and called "Absolutely not selling" over his shoulder without turning around.

Neither he nor Charlie said another word as they walked back to the house.

Chapter Two

"Another muffin?"

Dana looked up at the cheerful owner of the Gingham Pocket bed-and-breakfast where she was staying. The older Latina woman had a buoyant joy about her that sparkled out of her dark brown eyes with no effort at all. It was a good thing Dana was only here until she found a long-term rental because Rita Salinas's chocolate-cherry muffins were dangerous indeed. "I'll stick to one, thanks. But they are delicious."

Rita pulled a slip of paper out of the pocket of today's vintage apron—she had an impressive collection of them—and set it down next to Dana's coffee mug. Rita pointed to something written in curvy script. "Since you told me yesterday you were looking for a long-term rental, I talked to my friend, Marion," she said, tapping the address and phone number with a bright red fingernail. "She's heading up north to her son's for a while. You can rent out her place through the summer if you like. It's hot, but you get used to it." Rita had given Dana a nonstop tourism speech every day of her visit so far.

"Thanks. I'll give her a call."

"You can do better than that. Just walk on over there after breakfast. Marion's home and I told her you'd be in touch."

Dana felt a bit outmaneuvered, but she couldn't afford to stay in the B&B forever and it wasn't as if she had a stack of urgent appointments to keep. "Maybe I'll do just that."

Rita walked back to the sideboard and retrieved the coffeepot, returning to top off Dana's mug. "There is one thing about Marion's place you ought to know." She lowered her voice even though they were the only people in the room. "Marion's a lovely gal, honestly, but her place is…well… I expect most people would call it fussy."

"Fussy" turned out to be a dramatic understatement.

"Don't you worry. I'll unclutter it a bit between now and Friday, just to make the dusting easy on you," Marion promised.

Dana swallowed hard. Marion could unclutter between now and the end of the decade and only just start to come close to "open space." It wasn't exactly hoarding, but there were precious few flat surfaces not adorned with something. Several somethings. Dana tried to imagine what her colleagues at the precinct would say if they could see her future lodgings. They'd fall over laughing at the thought of stoic and sensible Dana Preston dusting froufrou figurines. And picture frames. And candy dishes. The number of throw pillows on the woman's couch alone boggled the mind.

Marion smiled as she adjusted a porcelain doe and fawn sitting on the coffee table. "I was so glad when Rita called. I always thought God would know exactly who should be in the house while I'm gone." She smiled at Dana. "Turns out, it's you."

Marion said the religious thought as if it were an ordinary thing, like a recipe or a shopping list. Maybe it was. If she was following the outrageous idea of coming here to help kids, maybe a little divine influence would be a welcome thing. After all, the only thing she knew for sure right now was that it looked as if only an act of God would convince Mason Avery to sell his land.

Mason stopped and stared at the gazebo in the town square Wednesday morning, a bit stunned that the striking blonde woman sitting in it was Dana Preston. His practical side told him to just keep walking. Charlie was back in school today and he had a million errands to run in town before heading back up the mountain. Still, the wary way she sat caught his attention—an odd mix of strength and unsteadiness, like someone used to being in control who suddenly isn't.

You've had enough experience at that to recognize it a mile off, he told himself. Some days, raising Charlie was like groping through the dark, looking for clues to a mystery you desperately needed to solve. Charlie was only a tiny bit happy, and Mason couldn't remember the last time he himself was anything close to happy. Most days it felt as if the legacy of the land and buildings around him were the only thing holding him together. The shaky faith he still clutched didn't pay the bills or assist with second-grade reading homework.

He allowed himself to watch her from a distance. The sharp angles of her haircut looked a bit out of place framing the soft features of her face. She was tall, but she didn't carry herself with a model's grace or the assertive elegance he associated with the two other real estate women who'd made inquiries about his land. Those women had treated him as little more than an obstacle in the way of their success. At least Dana had spoken to him like a human being, and not just a possible seller.

Just say hello, he told himself as he gave in to his curiosity and walked up to the gazebo. *You can be firm, but you don't have to be mean.*

"Hello." Not a grandiose greeting, but at least he'd managed to keep the suspicious edge out of his voice.

Her eyes widened in surprise, and Mason realized the reason they'd caught his attention yesterday. They were intense, yes, but they were an astoundingly clear green. A jade, sea glass kind of green. Even Charlie had said something about the color of her eyes. His son noticed the oddest things about people. Charlie also had a talent for latching onto the wrong people, so there was that.

"Hello," she replied, setting down the North Springs tourism brochure she was reading onto the stack already next to her on the gazebo bench.

"I'd like to know how you know so much about my property."

He waited for her to be offended at his directness.

She wasn't. "I do my research. I'm looking for a very specific kind of place."

Mason walked up the stairs to sit opposite her in the large octagonal structure. He tried to keep his voice even as he asked, "What about my land makes you think it's right for your…whatever you have in mind?" He remembered her description of a camp for kids, but he wanted to hear her explain it again. There was something in her voice and wording that kept snagging in his memory.

"I'd need land about the size of yours, with the buildings already in place. And I'd need someone already on-site who knows how to take care of it."

Mason's spine stiffened at the mention that her plans might include *him* in addition to his land.

"So yes, you tick all the boxes, if that's what you're asking," she went on.

I tick all the boxes? Not just the land? That was a new one. And more than a little unnerving.

"And like I said, it's for a camp," she continued. "A place for kids who have lost a parent to violence. Like Charlie."

Something about her saying Charlie's name poked his insides. "You researched how Melony died?" That felt like a violation of privacy even though it had been on the news and in the papers.

"Not until last night. After what I heard Charlie say to you. I didn't know that part." She swallowed and smoothed her hands on her knees—again—and he realized it was her sense of unsteadiness that stuck with him. After all, that same unsteadiness felt like his constant companion these days. "I'm sorry," she said, holding his gaze.

Lots of people had said "I'm sorry" to him over the past three years. He could tell when people really meant it. She did, but that didn't mean he was okay about it, or her.

Mason merely nodded, withholding the "thank you," he usually responded to people's condolences.

"How is Charlie taking it? How'd he process the trauma?"

Ordinary people didn't use words like "process the trauma."

"You a counselor or something?" Charlie had been through three of those—Mason was in no hurry to meet another.

The question seemed to push Dana off balance a bit. She pulled in a deep breath and sat back. "Police detective, actually. In Denver. I was—or still am. I'm sort of working that out."

He raised an eyebrow at how little sense her answer made. Of all the things he was expecting her to say, that wasn't anywhere on the list.

"I'm pretty sure I'm done with that. Actually, I know I am. I couldn't really take watching a kid's life fall to pieces anymore. I'd rather do what I can to keep the mess from happening in the first place."

That seemed a rather shiny way to put it. "With a camp?" She had to know how ridiculous that sounded.

"Yeah," she said, with a sheepish voice that told him she did, in fact, know how ridiculous the idea sounded. "With a camp."

Mason did not like how the idea sunk into him. Every bone in his body resisted the tiny molecule of sense it made as the answer to a bunch of his problems. What kind of woman with her background would dream up an idea like that? "I told you I'm not interested in selling."

That failed to soften the determination in her eyes. "You did." It was a challenge, not an agreement, and it lit a sort of emerald fire behind the sea-glass green in those eyes.

"So you'd best pack up and go home. Or find some other locale for your little happy ending story." The bitter edge in his words came so easily it shocked him. When had he become this mean?

Her chin rose in a defiance that put Charlie's to shame. "Actually, I just signed on to stay in Marion Gilbert's place clear through the summer." She dangled a set of keys on a rhinestone cactus key chain as evidence.

She *what*? Mason swallowed hard as he stood up. Did she think she was going to stick around in North Springs and somehow wear him down until he signed on to be a part of her dreamy-eyed mission? "Don't hold your breath, Ms. Preston."

She stood up as well, her height nearly placing them eye-to-eye. "You'll find I'm a remarkably patient person, Mr. Avery."

She'd set her mind to it. Which meant she'd set her mind to him. His skin buzzed with that realization as if he'd touched the electric fence on the west side of the property. "Why are you so bent on doing this? On *my* property? I mean, there have to be foundations, organizations... I don't know, charities that do this sort of thing. Why you?"

* * *

Dana looked at him for a moment, then she sat back down on the gazebo bench. He did the same. She'd have to tell him. "I worked juvenile violent crimes back in Denver."

"Juvenile violent crimes," he repeated. "Those words put together feels all kinds of wrong. But if you know about Melony, you already know life has taught me how all kinds of wrong it can be."

Dana felt a cinch in her heart—she had wounds, but he had a profound loss. She told herself to press on, to tell him the story he needed to hear. "Sometimes it was adults doing violence to kids. And that's awful enough. But kids being violent with each other? That's hard to swallow. I've seen some things that make you wonder if the world ought to still be turning."

She thought he would say something to push back against a remark like that. Most people did—but he didn't.

"Last fall, I worked a case where a nine-year-old shot his dad. *On purpose.*" She felt her shoulders tighten at the memory. "His dad beat his little sister one too many times and he'd had enough. Went into the box in the bottom of his dad's closet, got out the handgun and shot his dad in the shoulder. Mom was at work on the night shift and Dad was raging by the time the paramedics got there. The little guy had locked himself and his sister in the bathroom like he'd had to do it a million times."

"Seeing that would harden anybody," he offered. He was tall and broad shouldered but carried himself with a weariness that told her life had hardened him as well.

Maybe that's how he could see her own brittle spirit. "You know what the worst part of it was for me? How proud he was. A nine-year-old was boasting to us how he finally took his daddy down so he wouldn't hit him or his sister anymore. Not a shred of remorse. Not even any idea that there might be another option. Who gets that angry at that age?"

"I get that angry," Mason said as though it just slipped out without his permission. "I get angry that one annoyed man in a pickup truck cost my wife her life. Sure, she cut him off. Melony wasn't ever the best of drivers and I'm sure Charlie was distracting her." Mason's dark brown eyes glinted with a dark and angry edge. "She didn't do anything to deserve what he did. He hurled a wrench at her window so that it shattered and she drove off the road into a tree. You can't tell me anyone deserves that."

"I'm sorry," Dana said quietly. What else could be said?

"So you want to talk about angry? One night, I boiled over and threw a wrench of my own through our garage window. I hope Charlie never figures out it was me who did that."

They sat in silence for a moment, both pushing their way through the remembered pain.

Finally, he said, "You can't fix that with a camp. If that's why you're here, you ought to turn around right now."

"Well, it's only half the reason."

"What's the other half?"

"In January, I was on a call of shots fired. Between

two eleven-year-olds. Argument, gang initiation, it doesn't really much matter why. But they were staring each other down like some sort of cowboy gunfight when we got there. Both had cuts and bruises, so this was a case of fists escalating into something more."

She shifted in her seat. The story always made her skin crawl and grew a ball of ice in her stomach. "I moved in to try and de-escalate, and do you know they both turned and fired on me? I'm in there trying to keep them from killing each other and they're ticked off enough to turn on me." She let her hand come to rest on her abdomen. "Two bullets. They tell me it's amazing I survived."

"People always tell me I'm blessed that Charlie survived the crash. I know that's true, but it's hard to take a day that stole the love of my life, the mother of my child, and come out of it with anything I could call blessed." He gave a resigned shrug. "Mostly, I'm wrecked. Just trying to figure out how to keep going day by day."

The honesty of his admission returned just a bit of the warmth to his eyes. He had a handsome face, and looked as if he'd have a very disarming set of dimples if he ever smiled. Still, he bore the familiar weary appearance of a man who hadn't smiled in a long time.

"I couldn't keep going," she admitted in reply. "After the surgery and the recovery and everything, I knew I couldn't go back. I couldn't keep stomping out fires someone else had lit. And kept lighting. I needed to find a way to take away the matches."

He shook his head. "No offense, but I don't get it."

She had to find a way to make him understand. "All

three of those boys had already lost someone to a gun-
shot. They'd never known a life where people didn't
shoot each other. We gotta find a way to undo that. Heal
some of the wounds. Get them out of that world, even
if only for a short time."

Mason looked up at the mountains behind them
where she knew his land lay. "That's an awfully tall
order for twenty acres of land and one gutsy lady."

Dana felt herself smile just a little bit at the compliment Mason probably hadn't meant to give. "Yeah.
But I gotta start somewhere. I grew up near here, and I
found myself thinking of this place—the mountains, the
way the sky goes on, all the stars you can see at night—
during my rehab. Seemed like the place to start." She
fixed him with a direct, intense glare and asked the
one question she thought would drive her point home.
"Don't you ever worry that Charlie's growing up in a
world where people run moms off the road?"

There was a heavy, stretched-thin pause before
Mason answered, "Every. Single. Moment."

"I've got a plan of sorts drawn up. Nothing complicated, just a few charts and schedules." For a moment
she dropped her hard shell, hoping he'd see the ache in
her to do this outrageous thing. "Will you let me drop
them by?"

He thought about it for so long Dana was about to
give up hope, but then he sighed and said, "I suppose."

It wasn't exactly a yes, but it was close enough.

Chapter Three

Friday evening, Dana grabbed the tote bag that held her files and drawings off the passenger seat and stepped out of the car. The house in front of her was bigger than she'd guessed. A wide adobe structure with arches and several porticos, it gave the appearance of having been grand—once upon a time. Now chips in the paint and crumbling corners in some of the stucco told of neglect, or at least inattention. There were flower boxes under some of the windows and a set of stunning planters on either side of the impressive doorway, but all of them were empty.

The sense that came to her as she took in the landscape was a familiar one from her work: *this could be so much more*. It didn't happen all the time, but there were moments when she would see a child—or sometimes even a family—and would be hit with a bone-deep sense of *you could be so much more*. Potential seemed too institutional a word. Purpose came close. Something bright and shiny but still out of reach. Hope? The word kept hounding her thoughts.

"She's a big house, that's for sure," came Mason's voice from behind her. He was walking out of a garage-like building behind her, wiping his hands off on a blue bandanna. He looked less harsh than he had at the ga-zebo. Fit, strong, but not as defensive on his own turf.

The smell of sawdust and the collection of wood behind him in the building reminded her that Mason had a carpentry business. His website spoke of basic structural construction work, but there was also a sec-tion of beautiful furniture. He had an artistic side, a man who created with his hands. That artisan's skill wasn't visible anywhere in the overlooked beauty of the home in front of her.

"Nice house." *Probably beautiful in its day*, Dana added in her head. *Maybe beautiful again, if we can manage it*. Beauty and creativity had to be a part of the camp and was one of the reasons she'd felt drawn to Mason. Her idea for the place needed both natural beauty and pleasing accommodations. Too many of these kids came from ugly worlds where beauty was for other, more fortunate people. Her mind landed on the mem-ory of eleven-year-old Eddie from last summer. Eddie found two uses for the knife he always carried: one was to whittle amazing little figures, and the other was to cut himself. Getting Eddie into treatment was one of her favorite victories. Dana peeked at the graceful curves of a table leg in the shop behind Mason and thought, *What victories could Eddie discover in a place like this?*

Mason led her to the little dining room set while Charlie sat watching what sounded like cartoons in the next room. She wasted no time in battling his polite resistance with a pile of charts, drawings and tables.

"This house would be central, of course," she continued as she described her vision for the property as it was all marked out on an aerial shot of Mason's land. "Dining, gathering and any non-counselor staff. Not a ton of staff, by the way. This wouldn't be a large-scale operation. No more than twenty kids at a time. Less if we do surviving parent/child pairings, which I think would get the best results." She waited for his reaction at her use of the word "we."

He raised an eyebrow. "Twenty? And parents? You couldn't fit that in here."

"Well, no," she admitted. "That's why we'd need to take the two barns and turn them into multiple small bedrooms for kids and their parents. The two larger sheds could be dorms if we needed them and the greenhouse could be a gathering space, I think. Not sure about that yet."

A skeptical frown grew on his face. "You're talking about a lot of renovation."

"Maybe, but that's why I need someone with your skill set. You've got the only right combination of skills and layout in the county near as I can see."

"Just because I can doesn't mean I want to."

Dana fought the little voice of *you're beyond foolish to try this* that seemed to be her constant companion since she came to North Springs. She folded her hands on the table as resolutely as she knew how. "Well, no, not yet."

"But you're going to convince me. Or try to." Doubt-

ful didn't begin to cover his expression. Still, she chose
to see more challenge than outright refusal in his eyes.

"That's the plan, yes." She shifted the property drawing so that it faced him. "What are you doing with the
sheds and greenhouse right now?"

Dana wished she could gauge if her preparation and
persistence were getting her anywhere. Mason was so
hard to read. "Those buildings aren't in use at the moment." When she tried to make a comment about that,
he jumped to add, "I do have the right to use—or not
use—my own property as I please."

Dana forced herself to back down a bit. "You do. But
this is family property, isn't it? Charlie referred to the
house as 'Grandpa's house.'"

Ouch. That seemed to be a sore spot. "This land has
been in my family for three generations," he said curtly.
"It's going to stay that way."

"Is it?"

"What's that supposed to mean?"

Dana gave him as pointed a look as she dared. "Can
I spin a scenario out for you? Purely hypothetical. But
hear me out."

When he scowled but didn't outright refuse, Dana
took it as consent. "This is a big chunk of land," she
went on. "Prime land, and I expect from the gate, Charlie's attitude and your none-too-friendly welcome that
you've had your share of people coming at you to sell."

"I've had offers, yes."

She'd done her homework. She knew he'd received
offers and declined every one. "But this place won't
stay what it is now if you sell. They'll knock everything

down and put up condos or a resort or some other thing you really don't like. I won't do that. I'll use every building as intact as I can. We'll work together to make sure this stays as close to your father's land as possible. Nobody else can promise you that like I can."

Mason couldn't decide if it was a sign—good or bad—that she'd managed to hit on the one thing that bothered him most about selling. It felt like selling out. As if he was failing the long line of Avery men who'd put their backs into this land. As if he was failing Charlie and the legacy a man was supposed to leave his son.

"So I'm supposed to swallow the line that a camp is a better use than a spa or homes?" Even as Mason said it, the blatant truth of that hung in the air between them. A camp *was* a far better use of the land than a spa or condominiums. But it was still less of an option than keeping the land. He and Charlie living alone on twenty acres he could barely manage. Who was he kidding? He was *not* managing. The place was slowly falling into disrepair because he could only scrounge up enough money and willpower to survive, not to get ahead.

"Yes. Because it is. You want this land, this place to mean something. Nobody else is offering—nobody else *will* offer you the chance for this place to mean something this important. Changed lives. Saved lives. A tiny corner of the world you and I both know is far too broken to put back the way it ought to be." She seemed surprised by her own passion, as if she didn't know she had such lofty words within her.

Why couldn't the woman in front of him be an oily

salesperson instead of the memorable, wounded beauty
he could see too easily? And those eyes. Could everyone see the wounds in her eyes? Or did they just speak
that strongly to him?

"You seem awfully sure of yourself." He tried to
keep her impassioned words from digging into him
before he could put up enough resistance. It wasn't entirely working.

Dana paused for a long moment before replying,
"Not at all. Farthest thing from it. In fact, I have no
idea what I'm doing. Only that I have to do it. I've got
the why. But I'm counting on you to bring the how."

"Me?" Counting on him? Of all the ideas she'd posed
today, that one was perhaps the most outrageous.

She met his response with a shaky and endearing
sort of defiance. "Yeah, you. Because if this works the
way I'm planning, not only will the land matter, you'll
be crucial to it mattering. Well, don't know about you,
but I'm pretty sick of feeling like an insignificant speck
against the big wave of bad out there. You and I have
both had a hefty dose of that. Now I have to fight back,
because…well, because I just have to."

He'd felt that way once. Back when the grief hadn't
swallowed up all his fight and purpose, back when he
was a ball of anger railing against the world that took
Melony from him. "You're asking a lot here." The resistance should have come easier. He'd never planned
on saying yes today, but it was unsettling how far he
had to reach for the hard no he had in mind.

"I am." No apology or plea softened her tone. She
knew what she was asking and wasn't afraid to ask it,

despite the nerves he saw tighten her fingers. Dana Preston was making a very brave march out onto some very thin ice. Some part of him couldn't help but respect that. Maybe even be drawn just the tiniest bit toward it.

"Yes. And one more thing," she said as she rose out of the chair. The woman was tall and willowy, straight and strong. *Like a poplar tree*, he thought. *Good wood. Versatile, hard, easy to work with, doesn't split when you nail it.* He doubted she would take the comparison as the reluctant compliment it was.

Mason wasn't sure why he braced himself. "What?"

"Do you want Charlie to have a purpose in life? To grow up with a sense of direction, of value? For your son to know that he's more than just the survivor of a very sad accident?"

What kind of a question was that? "Of course I do," he answered loudly, probably a little defensively, but she'd earned that tone from him.

Dana pierced him with a glare so direct he felt it in the pit of his stomach. "You can't give what you don't have."

The phone rang just then, but he couldn't let that be the last word from her. "Give me a minute, will you? Charlie's watching TV in the den, maybe go say hello to him."

He ducked into the hallway as she wandered in the direction of Charlie and his television show. The name of Charlie's teacher Martha Booker came up on his phone screen, and he tamped down the tiny surge of alarm that always rose with calls from school or church. It was Friday night. What was so urgent it couldn't wait until Monday? "Hi, Martha, what's up?"

"I'm sorry I didn't call earlier, Mason, but I've been on the phone with a few parents smoothing things over. I'm wondering if you could come into school Monday morning. I need to speak with you and Charlie about what happened today."

The tiny surge blossomed into a tornado. "What happened?"

"Charlie hasn't said anything?"

"No. He's been a little on edge, but that happens a lot, still."

"There was an incident. He and Nathan Summers. It's something I think we need to nip in the bud before it gets more serious."

More serious. Those weren't comforting words. "What happened, Martha?" He remembered the scrape on Charlie's elbow. Why didn't he ask him how he got it?

"According to Mrs. Summers, Charlie threw a rock at their car window."

A rock. At a car window. The idea of it turned Mason's stomach. "He *what*?"

"Charlie and Nathan got into a scuffle over something in the playground earlier. Charlie responded by throwing a rock at their car after school before the kids were lining up for the bus. I don't know how any of the teachers missed it, but Mrs. Summers was understandably upset."

Mason couldn't fathom Charlie doing anything so violent, much less *that* particular act. "Are you sure it wasn't just a mistake?" He knew better even as the words left his mouth.

"Unfortunately, yes. Charlie missed on the first throw but tried two more times. The third one chipped the window. I'm sure you can understand why we're taking this very seriously. I wanted to make sure I had the facts from everyone before I upset you with a call like this."

Upset was an understatement. Mason leaned back against the hallway wall as a wave of dread washed over him. Charlie was going under. He'd been fighting like crazy to keep both their heads above water, to crawl their way to the shore of this sea of grief and loss, and it wasn't working. Charlie was drowning in the aftermath of what had happened to them.

Dana came back at that moment, ready to say something, but stopped wide-eyed at Mason's expression.

"I understand, Martha. I agree this is serious. And upsetting." He started to say "This is so unlike Charlie," but realized he couldn't. Charlie was sliding downhill, had been for a while, and he'd talked himself into ignoring it. The sense of failure pressed him against the wall.

"Would ten a.m. work?" the teacher asked.

"Absolutely. I'll do whatever you think is necessary." Mason's dry mouth and shocked brain could hardly form the words.

"Why don't you try and talk to Charlie about this over the weekend," Martha suggested. "See what he has to say about what happened and why."

"I will." How was he going to navigate this while he was barely holding it together himself?

"We're going to see Charlie through this, Mason. We're all behind you. Remember that."

Somehow Martha's kind words only made it worse. Mason let the phone fall on the hallway table—the one he'd built for Melony for her birthday four years ago—and covered his face with his hands.

"Mason…" Dana's words were low and cautious.

He didn't know how on earth to talk to Charlie about this. Still, Mason realized there was someone standing in front of him who did. Who'd maybe done it hundreds of times. He was too desperate to care about pride or the fact that he barely knew her.

Mason pulled his hands away from his face and stared into Dana's worried eyes. "Charlie's done something—something awful—and I think I need you to help me figure out why."

Chapter Four

"That doesn't sound much like Charlie to me," Dana replied when Mason gave her a quick rundown of the troubling facts. It didn't, but she'd also not seen nearly enough of the boy to make a fair assessment.

And even if she had, she'd seen some alarming transformations from some of the least likely candidates. The straight-A student who'd taken to keying cars in parking lots after his brother was killed in a hit-and-run accident. The sweet-as-pie toddler from the private school kindergarten who began biting everyone in her class when her father was killed in a mass shooting. Kids often processed enormous traumas in startling ways.

Mason looked shattered. "No, it doesn't. Charlie would never do something like that."

Dana dared a direct look. "No offense, but if I had a dollar for every time I heard that from a parent, I could open up my camp on a private island."

He scowled. "Not exactly helpful information."

This was going to be a tough conversation. It required a skill set she wished she didn't have, even though part of her was glad to be able to help Mason at a moment like this. The man looked lost and wounded—and beyond guilty. Whatever Charlie had done, Mason clearly blamed himself for it. She knew even really good kids could buckle under the weight of a traumatic experience. She told him that—twice—but he wasn't in a place where he could hear it.

An idea struck her. "Have you got any cookies?"

"What?"

"Cookies. Something for him to hold, to do, while we try and get the info out of him."

He looked as if he found that ridiculous. "Um, yeah."

"Okay. Grab a couple and meet me on the porch steps. Sit next to him and hand him a cookie."

"The porch steps?"

"Yes. Just trust me on this." If they were sitting on the porch steps looking up at the view, Charlie wouldn't feel cornered and didn't have to look anyone in the eye. "Ask him to tell you what happened. See if you can get him to give you his version before anyone gets into accusations."

When he hesitated, she pressed, "Mason, I know what I'm doing here. You asked me to help. So let me help."

Settled in a few minutes later with two cookies each on the front steps, Dana caught Mason's eye over Charlie's head. She nodded for him to start.

"Charlie," Mason said, bumbling a bit, "Mrs. Booker called me about what happened at school today. Can you tell me what happened?"

"Nothing happened," Charlie mumbled.

Mason caught her gaze over Charlie's head again, but Dana nodded to keep going. She had been fully expecting Charlie's answer.

"Something must have happened if Mrs. Booker wants me to come in Monday and talk about it. I really need you to tell me so I can help sort this out."

"Nathan's mean." Charlie's pronouncement was soft and wounded.

Mason sighed. "Kids can be mean. Sometimes they don't even realize they're being mean."

"What did Nathan do that made you so mad at him?" Dana asked. It was better to couch it in terms of Charlie's anger than on how mean and violent he'd been. Kids Charlie's age didn't always know how to handle so much anger. How much anger must still be boiling around in that little chest after what he'd been through?

She took a bite of cookie as Charlie paused for over a minute before answering, "Said something about Mom."

Dana could almost hear Mason's flinch of pain. She'd long since stopped pretending the world was a just place, but the burden he was forced to carry seemed beyond unfair. "What did Nathan say about Mom?" Mason's back stiffened as if readying himself for the blow.

Charlie's lower lip jutted out. "He asked me if I had to skip school on Special Ladies Day because I don't have a mom anymore."

I'm pretty sure Mrs. Booker didn't hear that part, Dana thought. Also, what on earth was Special Ladies Day?

"He said it all mean-like," Charlie added.

"He might have, or maybe you just heard it mean-like," Mason replied. "Some people don't understand how talking about Mom still hurts a lot." His simplified words held a world of pain behind them. "And Grandma's coming in from Flagstaff for Special Ladies Day, remember?"

Dana thought the event sounded a bit ridiculous. In her world something like that would be fishing for disappointment and heartache. Most of the kids she dealt with would be hard-pressed to come up with any adult friend, much less sort them out by gender.

Charlie broke his cookie in two and stuffed one half in his mouth. "Willy," he said with his mouth full, "He's that fourth grader I told you about? He said I should be mean right back to Nathan."

I've met a hundred Willys and they all think that way, Dana thought.

"I don't think that's true," Dana said. "Most people are nice if you're nice to them. Not all, but most." Still, poking at a raw spot could egg on even the most even-tempered adult, much less a sad little boy. "Has Nathan been mean before?"

Charlie kicked the back of the porch step with his heel. "He asks me stupid questions."

"Like…" Mason replied.

"Who packs my lunch." *Poking at a raw spot indeed*, Dana thought.

"I do," Mason said. He said it so matter-of-factly that Dana wondered if he'd done it before his wife's passing. He seemed to be a highly involved father even before life forced all of the parenting on his shoulders.

"Nathan says *moms* do that kind of stuff."

"I know plenty of dads who pack lunches," Dana replied, even though she could only name two at the moment. "Maybe Nathan just doesn't know any." She decided to lean in and risk catching Charlie's gaze. "And that *was* kind of a nasty question. But I think we ought to talk about the rocks."

Charlie's wide eyes broadcast his fear and guilt.

"Did you throw rocks at Nathan's car window?" She added just enough of her *don't mess with me* tone to get a straight answer out of Charlie. The guys back at the department called it her secret weapon—the "mom factor" one of them even called it. Given the circumstances, that was sadly poetic, but a tactic was a tactic when necessary.

"I'd rather hear it from you," Mason said. "We need to fix this."

Charlie nodded. "He made me so mad," he grumbled, sounding on the verge of tears.

Dana's mind cast back to a fourteen-year-old standing over the mangled wreck of his neighbor's bike. The kid had taken a baseball bat to it over a tiny remark. Turns out the boy's father had sold his own bike the week before to pay for booze. The boiling point of anger and tears sounded just the same. Why was it so hard to get people to understand that violence was only the tip of the whopping iceberg underneath?

"Charlie." Exasperation filled Mason's tone as he pushed himself up off the stairs. It cinched at her heart to see a father at the end of his rope. The depth of his care and worry showed all over his face. "You can't do stuff like that. Even when you're mad."

Charlie needed to know they were on his side. "It just sort of burns up inside of you, doesn't it? And then it's hard to hold it back," Dana said.

The boy looked up at her, surprised she seemed to understand. "I just wanted him to stop asking dumb questions."

And stop saying painful things, Dana translated in her head. "It's really hard, I get it. And it's not fair that you have to." She looked at Mason. "You or your dad. But he's right, you have to find a way that isn't like what just happened."

"Willy said he'd beat up anybody who said anything about Mom. I told Nathan that."

"Oh, I'm sure that helped." Mason put a hand to his forehead and looked up at the sky.

"Maybe Willy's answer isn't the best one," Dana replied. She was glad to be here, helping these two find their way out of this. To be honest, she liked the two of them more than she wanted to admit. Just because she didn't carry a badge at the moment didn't make that urge to help set things right go away. "Maybe there's someone else we can ask for help." Only after the words left her mouth did she realize she'd said "we."

"A teacher, maybe?" Surely the school had assigned a counselor to Charlie at some point.

"Willy says teachers are dumb."

Mason rolled his shoulders and closed his eyes. Dana could see him fight back the frustration he was feeling. "Why are you suddenly listening to Willy? Mrs.

Booker is nice. And she cares about you. And she's as worried as I am about these choices you're making all of a sudden."

There were times when the objectivity of not being mom or dad was a gift. Fond as she was of Charlie, she wasn't as emotionally charged by this chain of events as Mason was. It enabled her to see things, to ask questions, to make connections that people closer to the situation were often too upset to recognize.

Pretty sure this was one of those times, Dana leaned over and hugged her knees as she sat on the steps. It put her face even with Charlie's scrunched features as the boy stared at his feet. "Can you tell me why it's so much harder now?" she asked softly.

The question seemed to knock the air out of Mason's frustration. "Friday," he answered before the boy even spoke. With a regret-filled moan, he sunk down on the steps beside his son. "Next Friday. Aw, Charlie, how did I forget that? How did I not see that coming?"

Charlie looked up at his dad, small and wounded. The boy didn't say a word, but his teary eyes said everything. Mason pulled him into a hug and made a sound close to a mournful wail.

"Oh, Charlie, I'm so sorry I didn't remember. I can't believe I didn't remember."

Watching the fresh wound open up on Mason's face sent a sharp blade to Dana's insides. This was clearly far beyond forgetting to send a card or some other small oversight. Mason looked utterly heartbroken, making Dana feel as if she'd intruded on a deeply painful moment. She didn't know these people well enough to be here, and yet there was a startling power in being here. A service, a protection she was uniquely qualified to give. After all, she'd seen the absolute worst in people. She'd seen depths of neglect and lack of caring that could make a person's blood run cold. If anything, the scene in front of her was all about so much care. Loads of care with no place to go. A dad torn apart by trying so, so hard.

"I'm sorry," Mason mumbled into Charlie's hair, clutching the boy tight. Dana thought maybe she ought to go but didn't dare move and ruin the moment. "I'm so sorry. It's hard, and I'm not getting it right, am I?"

You are, Dana wanted to shout to him, *You care, and that's so much of getting it right.* At that moment, if the only thing her project ever did was give Charlie and Mason a foothold toward their future, she'd make the whole thing happen just for them. A fierce loyalty to them seemed to spring up out of thin air, illogical and probably foolhardy.

Was next Friday this Special Ladies thing? All this seemed to be about something bigger than that. Still, Dana kept silent, not daring to ask.

"How are we gonna do it, Dad? The pond is gone. Mom is gone and now the pond is gone." His small voice pitched high with worry. The day was obviously special in some way, and combined with Nathan's crack about Special Ladies Day, it wasn't hard to see what had sent Charlie over the edge. Still, Dana didn't ask, just waited to see if Mason would explain.

After swiping one of his own eyes with the back of his hand, Mason seemed to remember she was there and hoping for an explanation. "Melony," he began with an unsteady voice, "My late wife and Charlie's mom— was Hawaiian."

"Mi-li-lani," Charlie said carefully. "That was her other special name."

Suddenly the tropical touches Dana had seen around the house made sense. They had seemed a little out of place in the middle of the Arizona desert at first, but now they struck her as important touches to the home.

"Melony's parents always honored the people gone in their family by sending a lei out onto the water on a certain day in April. That was a bit hard to pull off here, so we kept the tradition up by sending a little ring of flowers out across the pond on the west side of the property."

"It's all dried up," Charlie said. "It's just mud with cracks in it now."

One more thing life had taken away from Charlie Avery. Dana felt like driving to the nearest hardware store and the florist to pick up a wading pool and a bouquet of flowers right this minute—further proof of this new impulsive nature she'd somehow gained. Not that it would even come close to setting it right, but surely there was something that could be done. "There's got to be other water somewhere else. It's still a week away, we can figure something out."

Charlie's frown turned Dana's gut inside out, and from the looks of it, Mason's sense of despair wasn't far behind. "It's supposed to be on *our* pond. It's always been on our pond."

Mason tightened his arms around Charlie. "I know, Charlie. I know."

Dana could not let it end with that hopelessness. "Charlie, was your mom a problem solver? Did she find ways to fix things?"

Charlie squinted at her. "Dad fixes things."

Dana tried again. "Your dad fixes things, but do you think your mom was the kind of person who fixed problems? Skinned knees, nightmares, missing toys, *people* kinds of things?"

The boy wiped his nose on his sleeve. "Yep."

"So, seems to me she'd want you to find a way to fix this. Figure out a way to solve the problem of having this day without your pond. Kind of a tough problem, but you seem like a smart kid to me."

"I'm good at math." Dana was glad to see a tiny spark of the former Charlie return to the boy's eyes. Every law enforcement officer knew the moment a situation tipped back from escalating into something worse. Dana felt that familiar pop of relief in her chest.

"And she'd probably think that the rocks weren't the way to solve it, am I right?"

Charlie nodded reluctantly.

"So now that we know what the real problem is, we can figure out a way to solve it. The right way, like your dad said. Are you up for it?"

"I s'pose."

"And that probably has to start with saying 'I'm sorry' to Nathan and his mother."

The horror of that showed on Charlie's face. "Do I hafta?"

"Yes, you *hafta*," Mason said. The look of at-my-wit's-end gratitude on his face burrowed itself into Dana's heart. It felt very much like the first bit of the healing she was coming here to find. He managed a struggling smile.

"You've still got flowers, right? There's some right over there I can see. We'll just have to find ourselves a stunt pond to fill in until your pond fills back in."

Mason laughed. "A *stunt* pond?" The dimples she had suspected showed up and completely changed his face. He was indeed a handsome man when the darkness lifted—even if only for a moment.

"Well," she replied with a laugh herself, "Isn't it?"

"That's goofy," Charlie said. "*You're* goofy."

It was the nicest thing anyone had said about her in a very long time.

Mason was feeling a million things at once as he walked Dana to her car. Nothing today had gone the way he'd expected. While part of him was grateful, a larger part of him felt totally lost. Like a compass wheel that had lost its magnetic north, spinning in any number of unhelpful directions.

His distress must have been obvious, because Dana looked at him for a long moment before asking, "Are you going to be okay?"

He ran a hand through his hair. "I don't actually know. Rocks? At a car window? How can Charlie even think to do something like that? Given what happened to him?"

Dana leaned against the car. "That's just it—he's not thinking. He's reacting, grabbing at whatever seems to make sense in the moment. I'm no counselor, but I've seen it enough times." She sighed. "I've been on the receiving end of it enough times."

Mason pointed back toward the house where Charlie was upstairs getting ready for bed. "He's turning into this whole other boy I don't even recognize." He tried to stop the words from gushing out, but they pushed at him with such force. "I feel like I'm losing him," he choked out.

It stung—hard—to admit that. The words hung in the quiet night air, raw and condemning. Mason found he wanted to hear what Dana would say to that, mostly because he knew he wasn't going to get some trite assurance from her. Now that rocks had been hurled at a car window—by his *own son*—the time for trite assurances had passed them by.

"You haven't lost him," Dana said. "But you might. He's lost his moorings and he's looking for them in all the wrong places."

"You mean like that Willy kid."

"Look, I'm not saying Charlie's going to run out and join a gang. But you need to know that's how it starts. Kids looking for something solid to grab onto. Somewhere to belong, teammates, a connection. Mind if I tell you something? Something that will sound like it doesn't apply, but it does?"

Mason didn't know how to answer a question like that. "Okay, I guess."

"We have a great big mall out by where I live. Every year we have a joint meeting with the mall security to go over emergency action plans, hangout spots, kids to watch out for, that sort of thing. The chief of security told me once that he always tells parents to teach their kids to go up and ask a stranger for help if they get separated. Another parent, hopefully, but to pick someone who looks helpful. The total opposite of the 'don't talk to strangers thing.'"

Encouraging kids to talk to strangers? That was a new one. "Why?"

Dana fixed him with a stare he felt sink down to the pit of his stomach. "Because statistically speaking, that child is far better off with someone they approach than someone who approaches them. Someone who might be seeking out a lost and vulnerable child."

Mason felt his blood run cold. Dana's words held a mirror up to him, and he didn't much care for what he saw. For someone trying to convince him to go along with her ideas, she wasn't coddling or smooth-talking him one bit—just the opposite, in fact. "What are you saying?"

"I'm saying that there's protection, and there's hiding. Charlie needs a better sort of friend than Willy, and he's not going to find it hiding up here on the mountain. The camp could bring some new friends to him, but I think we just found out you haven't got that long. You've got to rejoin the human race right out there in front of him."

He didn't know what to say to that. Actually, he did. "What's the next step in figuring out if this camp thing is even possible?"

Dana was as shocked by Mason's question as he was. Still, he knew she had an answer in that thick file they'd never even opened tonight. "Zoning and building code requirements."

"Okay, look into it."

Her whole face changed. "Really? We haven't even…"

He held up one hand. "I'm not saying yes. I'm saying look into it. I didn't get to hear the speech I expect you had prepared, but it seems my own son made your point for you."

She nodded. "Okay then."

Something shifted between them. A wall of sorts had come down—maybe not all the way, but partly. Mason found he wasn't on guard against her anymore. She'd proved herself to be on his side tonight, and he owed her an open mind for it.

He owed her something else. "Thank you. For helping me tonight. I was at the end of my rope and you kept me from…well, from losing my cool."

"You've still got to get through Monday with Mrs. Booker. That probably won't be much fun."

No, it wouldn't be anything close to fun. "But I'm in a better spot to do it because of how you helped me to talk to Charlie tonight. I'm grateful for that."

Her smile was bittersweet. There was something comforting about someone else who found themselves somewhere they didn't want to be. Another soul just trying to make the best of a rug yanked out from underneath them. Wildly off-balance was a lonely place to be. So many people had offered him all kinds of help from their solid, compassionate lives. He appreciated that, he really did.

But something about Dana's own brokenness gave him permission to be his own broken self. A deep grace from a woman who seemed to have no faith at all. There was a sort of wonder in that. It had been so long since he felt a sense of wonder about anything.

"You're welcome," Dana said softly. "Tell Charlie good-night for me, and I'll be thinking of you Monday."

It slipped into his mind before he could tell himself it wasn't appropriate: *I'll be thinking of you, too.*

Chapter Five

Dana tried to give Charlie and Mason space over the weekend so that they could work things out between themselves. She explored the town, some of the mountain trails, and busied herself with project paperwork.

By Sunday night, however, worry over the school meeting and the whole project kept her wide awake. She'd spent the last hour tucked under Marion's guest bedroom's ruffly bedspread staring at the lace canopy overhead. *Me. Here. How did that happen?* It seemed impossible to imagine anyplace so opposite of her life or her personality. This was a dainty, fussy house, and Dana Preston was not a dainty, fussy woman. Anything but. *What was I thinking?*

She ought to have turned on the lights as she made her way downstairs. That would have been smart, given the sheer terror she felt over knocking something over in this home. If a single figurine fell to the ground, Dana felt sure it would start a chain reaction and send dozens of things tumbling to the floor. Marion had been so nice. So trusting and somehow sure that Dana was *the* person to take care of this stuffed-full house while she was gone. *I can't break anything. I'll just have to be careful.*

She fretted over Charlie's well-being. Those skinny little shoulders were far too small to be bearing the kinds of burdens life had handed him. And Mason? The man was buckling under the strain of trying to guide his son while healing from his own grief. *I know grief never listens to any timetable, but it's been years. Shouldn't he have his feet more underneath him by now?*

But, what did she know? She'd never lost anyone who meant as much to her as Mason's late wife clearly meant to him. The painful truth was that she herself had never meant that much to anyone to be grieved so powerfully. To be so loved, to be so missed. She'd always prided herself on her fierce independence, but looking at Mason and Charlie opened up a yearning to be *that* loved. The longing only sharpened her sense of loss at the children she would now never bear. *How do you fill a hole that big? Where's the way forward through something like that?*

Dana was just congratulating herself for making her way through the dark house without incident when she ran smack into something hard. It fell over in front of her, taking her down with it. She cried out as the unmistakable sound of cracking wood filled her ears and a sharp pain ran across her shin.

"What have I done?" she asked the empty room as she limped to the wall and began reaching around for wherever the light switch might be. A full minute and several pained grunts later, Dana snapped on the light to reveal a bleeding shin and a kitchen chair with one leg snapped off. She'd damaged Marion's furniture. One more broken thing in her life, one more piece of damage she had no idea how to fix.

No sense attempting sleep now. After cleaning herself up with a paper towel and some ice, Dana sunk into one of the three remaining chairs. Stuffed with decorations as the house was, it still felt dark, empty and lonely in the middle of a sleepless night.

She needed something to calm herself. Tea? She usually stuck to coffee—but she'd seen that Marion had a teapot and a large assortment of teas. Deciding anything was worth a shot, Dana got up and hobbled to the cabinet.

She jumped back a bit when a church hymnal tumbled out of the cabinets from beside the boxes of tea bags. "Who keeps a hymnal with their tea?" Dana asked aloud as she scrambled to catch the book before it fell to the floor. Someone who couldn't sleep, came the oddly logical answer. After all, lots of people found hymns and prayers as comforting as chamomile. Rita and her husband Bart probably were. Perhaps even Mason. Everyone she'd met so far mentioned attending the picturesque church she'd seen a block off the square.

Dana filled the small kettle—just the right size for one, she noticed, as was the delicate little teapot. The dozen or so mugs she'd had in her cabinets at home were functional, but there was something truly soothing about a warm cup of tea in one of Marion's many elegant cups and saucers.

While she waited for the water to boil, Dana sat down and paged through the well-worn hymnal. It was old, with frayed bindings and whisper-thin pages. Several of them were flagged as favorites with the corner turned down—yet another of Marion's many collections.

Suddenly she was a young girl, swinging her legs in a church pew, accepting mints from her mother to keep the fidgeting at bay. Some familiar titles brought back foggy memories of tunes. Others, she'd never heard of but found the words poetic. People of faith turned to hymns as much as scripture, she supposed. The melodies stuck to the soul, for even she could recall a few after so many years. She'd seen a mother rock the body of her gunshot-wounded son and sing for her Lord to "take my hand" despite the fact that the young man was nearly twenty and twice her size. He'd died before the ambulance could arrive, and she kept humming the hymn long after they had loaded the body onto the gurney.

The words on the next flagged page caught Dana with a power she wasn't ready for. It spoke of a mercy that struck her as exactly what was missing from the world—even Charlie's sadly dried-up pond. But it was the verse about being "prone to wander" that pierced her. She'd somehow wandered off the course of her life. Or been pushed off by a pair of bullets sunk into her—did it matter which?

Was Mason a wanderer, too? Needing grace, needing God to pull him back from the abyss he seemed stuck inside? It all seemed too great a challenge for any person to face alone. She wanted so badly to help Charlie—to help a whole lot of Charlies—but all her yearning couldn't come close to matching the enormity of the problem. If she thought about it too much, helplessness swallowed her up.

Can You save him if I can't?

It wasn't really a prayer. It was more like a moan of her heart, raw and wordless like the humming of that grieving mother.

The kettle whistled. Dana poured the water into the pot, stilling to let the scent waft up to meet her breath. She set the pot down on the table next to the cup and saucer, and the open hymnal. While the tea steeped and filled the air with comfort, Dana ran her fingers over the verses, hearing the music in the silence. It wasn't really praying for Mason and Charlie—God would surely see through the ruse of that in a heartbeat given her own forgotten faith. Still, it was something close to prayer. Maybe God could take a broken intention and transform it into a prayer. Surely He cared enough about Charlie to do that.

As she drank her second cup of tea, Dana found a little index in the back of the hymnal, listing songs by their subject matter. She found several more hymns listed under "Asking for Guidance." Songs with words like "lead me" and "guide me," and two that took the familiar words of Psalm 23 and set them to music. Dana ran her fingers over each of the verses, sending the touch of them up to Heaven on Charlie's and Mason's behalf. It was silly, but it calmed her. Something much closer to peace than anything she'd known since the shooting settled in her soul.

What do you know? I still have a soul. Funny how she'd either forgotten it, or considered it long gone.

As she yawned, Dana reminded herself of the one enormous victory of the weekend: Mason had agreed to let her move forward on the exploration of turning his property into a camp. Would he have done that if the business with Charlie hadn't happened? Is that really how grace worked—bringing good out of bad and brokenness?

Tomorrow she would go to the town hall offices and look up all the zoning and building codes. And if the complexity of it all got to her, she'd stop and think about some of the words she read tonight. She might even get brave and say a prayer or two for guidance. After all, if she was willing to pray for Charlie and Mason, could she find the nerve to pray for herself and the camp? She would remember to check in with Mason, too, to see how the school meeting went.

It wasn't much of a plan—only for the next twenty-four hours, if she were honest, but it was a start.

Dana found a trio of Band-Aids in the kitchen drawer and patched up the long scrape on her leg. Then she wrapped her bathrobe around herself and headed back to bed. As she turned out the kitchen light, she left the hymnal open on the table where she could see it again in the morning.

It had been a bear of a morning.

After a grueling hour with Martha Booker in the

school counselor's office feeling like the Worst Parent Ever, Mason indulged in a luxury he hadn't allowed himself in a long time—a heaping plate of enchiladas at Guerro's. It wouldn't really solve anything—he knew that—but the fire of Guerro's diablo hot sauce might burn off a little of the helpless feeling that had been following him around all weekend. At any rate, it was a better tactic than calling Dana. He wasn't ready for how much he wanted to check in with her, to get her take on the tough conversations he'd had this morning. Bringing her headlong into his problems with Charlie might not be the smartest thing to do at the moment.

"Good to see you, stranger," Nicco Guerro greeted him. Melony had always called Nicco "a wonderful mix" of his father's Mexican heritage and his mother's Italian ancestry. The man raised an eyebrow as he set down the bottle of his spiciest sauce that was Mason's favorite. "The usual?"

"Please." Mason felt like every ounce of his weariness showed up in the words.

"How are you?" Nicco asked. "I mean, no offense, but you don't look so good. Still hard, hmm?"

Still hard. If Mason had to sum up his life in two words, those would be the two he chose. At least today. Which was shortsighted—and rather ungrateful—of him. He had several things to be thankful for in his life, even though every day felt like an uphill battle.

A bowl of chips and salsa appeared on the counter in front of Mason. "You don't come down off the mountain nearly as much as you used to. What brings you into town today?"

"School meeting. Charlie's made a couple of—" he used Mrs. Booker's teacherly sounding words "—poor choices."

Nicco laughed. "I made a whole lot of those." It was good to see him, and the man's checkered past was one of the reasons Mason sought him out after this morning. Nicco had gone far astray as a young man—crime, alcohol, prison, and that's just what Mason knew about—but had come back around to a solid life. "Don't recall making them in second grade, though." Nicco handed the order for the enchilada platter to the cook behind him, and then leaned forward toward Mason. "What'd *churro* do?"

It had been a while since Mason had heard Nicco use the nickname harkening back to the sugary, fried dough sweet. Charlie wasn't looking too sweet today, even though Mrs. Booker had made huge progress with the boy.

"Threw a rock and hit Nathan Summers's car window."

Mason recognized the flinch Nicco made at the words. He'd been flinching all morning himself anytime anyone mentioned it. Charlie couldn't have picked anything more particularly, singularly awful than what he'd done. It sunk down into Mason's soul that his son must know that on some level. Was it a giant call for help? Or just a big swing at a cruel world?

Nicco grunted his commiseration. "Tough one. And I can just imagine Brenda Summers's reaction. You got a handful there. Talk to her yet?"

"Oh, yeah." That had been the worst part. Brenda

Summers looked at Mason like he'd lost the battle for his son. A resigned sympathy coupled with a "keep your distance" coldness Mason felt to his bones. He couldn't bring himself to be upset with the woman because he didn't blame her one bit. He'd skipped church Sunday, mostly feeling like yellow caution tape ought to be put up around whatever pew they sat in. *Damaged family. Keep a safe distance.*

"Boys get over that stuff. I socked Joey Kingston in the mouth and broke his tooth in the sixth grade. Stood up in his wedding ten years later. You'll laugh about this someday."

"Not today," Mason sighed. "Not this month." Maybe not this year.

The door to the little diner pushed open, and of all people Dana Preston walked in. "I saw your truck out front," she confessed. "Thought maybe I'd catch you to ask how the morning went."

"He ordered the diablo hot sauce. That should tell you all you need to know," Nicco said, raising a *who's the pretty lady?* eyebrow at Mason.

Mason offered a helpless nod, half grateful she'd wanted to ask, half loath to tell her. "Have you had lunch yet?" felt like the best dodge he could come up with.

The barest hint of a smile turned up one corner of her mouth when she said, "No. And evidently bureaucracy makes me hungry."

She must have hit a roadblock—or six—in her exploration of the legalities for the camp. He was half-relieved. If the path had cleared itself in front of this project, he'd have to consider it more seriously. That felt impossible given everything on his plate at the moment.

"You have come to the best place to be hungry," Nicco said as he pulled out the chair opposite Mason and handed Dana a menu. "Tell me what you like and I'll tell you what to order."

Dana gave a huge, frustrated sigh. "What has the most cheese? Like, the *most* cheese?"

The amusing nature of her request broke the ice. Mason laughed and said, "The double quesadilla. With extra queso."

Nicco grinned. "He speaks the truth. So, you two know each other?"

"This is Dana Preston. She's new in town. Staying at Marion's place." Offering any more than that seemed too complicated for how he felt at the moment.

"Hello, Dana Preston. Welcome to North Springs. The most cheese we got, coming right up. Maybe you can cheer up my friend, yes?"

When Nicco retreated back behind the counter, Dana asked, "How'd it go?"

Mason tried to think of a simple way to sum up his difficult morning. "It went."

"That bad?"

"Everybody was very nice, said all the appropriate things, expressed buckets of concern. But my son threw a rock that chipped a car window. Not too many ways it could have gone other than how it did." Mason exhaled. "Charlie realizes he made a whopping mistake. That's something. I just don't know if we can keep it— or something like it—from happening again."

"You can," Dana said. Her words held a confidence Mason didn't feel. "He's young."

"He's too young to do what he did."

Dana sat back in her chair. "I could say that about most of the kids I arrested. Influence is as much of a weapon as a handgun, if you ask me." Mason watched her brow furrow as she noticed the music playing in the diner. "Dean… Martin? That's unexpected."

Mason was pleased to manage a laugh. "Nicco's mom was Italian. He's got a thing for Vegas lounge singers." Nicco's complex personality was one of the things Mason liked most about the man. "Speaking of influence, I told Charlie he can't sit with that Willy kid on the bus or hang out with him anymore."

Dana didn't look as impressed as he hoped. "That might backfire."

"Do you have a better idea?" Mason asked, and then immediately added, "Oh, wait, what was I thinking? Of course you do."

"I was going to say," she replied with that long-suffering tone women seemed to master so easily, "that forbidding something usually makes it more appealing."

Nicco returned and set down Mason's plate in front of him. Dana stared at the bold tattoo on Nicco's left arm, then looked up at him. "How'd you get out of the gang?"

Nicco stilled and returned Dana's stare. She'd surprised him, that was certain. Dana Preston didn't mince words with anyone.

"Law enforcement," she explained. "Denver PD, but some things are the same all over."

Nicco nodded, impressed. Mason thought that was a rather gutsy move on Dana's part, but then again, Dana was a gutsy woman. Nicco had never made a secret of the challenges of his past, but Mason wondered how the man would respond to so bold a question.

Nicco touched the tattoo and then the thick silver cross that hung around his neck. "Jesus and the love of a good woman."

Dana smirked. "Sounds like a mushy movie."

"Played out just like one, too," Nicco replied. "We've been married twelve years next month." He put his hand to his heart, dramatic and romantic. "*Mi vida*, that woman."

Tony Bennett began singing about leaving his heart in San Francisco over the speakers, and Mason could only offer a *what can I say?* shrug.

"Nice to see a happy ending to a story like that." The tone of her words told Mason she found such happy endings painfully rare. He wasn't much of a believer in happy endings himself these days. Perhaps that was why Dana's not-so-subtle lecture about pushing himself to get involved again with the community struck home.

"So, bureaucracy, huh? And here I was hoping your morning went better than mine." Mason wanted to bite back those words, realizing he had just admitted he'd been thinking about her and the tasks she hoped to accomplish this morning.

Dana's face fell. "I don't know which mountain is higher—the one you live on or the zoning codes and ordinances I have to navigate."

He'd suspected that—was even counting on it on some level. It couldn't be as easy as she seemed to make

it out to be. Her pie-in-the-sky attitude about the camp
seemed so out of place in her sensible personality. *What
makes a wild idea take a hold of someone like Dana
Preston?* Mason found himself leery of it and drawn
to it at the same time.

"Is it even possible?" he dared to ask carefully. He
didn't want to give her the impression he was sold on
the idea. If he even hinted how the idea was growing
on him, she'd take that and run with it. He felt an unsettling obligation to her now that she'd helped so much
with Charlie. That was fortunate timing—maybe God's
timing—but he wasn't ready to believe God was paving
the way to turn his family property into some camp.

Dana pushed out a long breath. "Complicated, but
possible." It was the first time he'd seen her confidence
falter. She'd been so bent on persuading him before now
that the crack in her warrior shell did things to his insides. "It's going to take…a lot."

He'd known that. And Mason wasn't at an "a lot"
place in his life right now. Getting through second grade
intact didn't leave a father with a lot of extra energy for
epic projects.

"I'm sorry," he said, just because she seemed so de-
jected. He wasn't sorry. Was he?

The sympathy seemed to jolt her back to her usual
self. "Don't be," Dana said with forced determination.
"I just have to get my head around it. I just need a plan,
and I'll make one."

You'll need way more than that, Mason thought to
himself. It struck him that he'd had the same view of his
own chances of getting Charlie into the third grade after

his morning meeting at school. Once more—despite his own efforts to ignore the idea—the thought came to him that they might both be needing the same answer. That was a thought that shook him to the bones.

Dana looked out the window. "I… I sort of need a favor."

She was already asking him to consider selling his land and she wanted *a favor*? "What's that?" His question was a bit sharper than it ought to have been.

Embarrassment flushed her features. "I fell over one of Marion's chairs last night and broke a leg off. Do you think you can fix it? I'll pay whatever you need to charge."

He wasn't expecting anything so practical. "Sure, I can take a look at it."

"It's in the back of my car. It's one of the reasons I came in here when I saw your truck out front." She said it as if wanting to see him and find out about Charlie was an off-base reason to come find him. He didn't like the way that itched under his skin.

"I fix furniture. It's what I do. I expect I can fix your chair." He surprised himself by adding, "I sort of owe you anyway, after what you did with Charlie."

"I get people in trouble to talk about what they did," she replied, a warm relief lighting her eyes. "It's what I do."

"Do you have the leg that broke off?" Somehow he knew she did. She seemed like a woman who never left loose ends.

"Yep."

It felt good to be able to do something for her. It

leveled the balance of obligation he felt after her assistance the other night. He didn't want to feel obligated to her in any way as he considered her plans for that camp of hers.

"We'll put it in my truck after lunch. I can probably have it back to you tomorrow if it's not too complicated a repair."

She looked surprised. "Really?"

Of course he couldn't be sure, but Mason also wasn't going to admit that he had a lot of spare time while sleep eluded him. Friday was coming, and he still hadn't figured out how to get Charlie through Melony's water ceremony without a pond.

"There's a barbecue in the town square Wednesday night. Charlie and I are thinking of *rejoining the human race* and going." He emphasized the words she'd lectured him with earlier. "I can bring it back to you then." He hadn't planned on making an offer like that. He didn't need to see her again this week—maybe he shouldn't see her again this week. Why did this woman muddle his thinking?

"That'd be great," she said with a surprising simplicity.

"Besides," he said for no good reason, "I've heard about Marion's house, but I've never seen the inside. Why pass up a chance like that?"

Nicco set down a heaping plate of food in front of Dana. Her eyes widened with delight, and Mason felt himself smile.

"There you have it," declared Nicco. "All the cheese any good-hearted woman could ever hope to eat. *Provecho*."

"I hope that means enjoy your cheese," Dana said with a grin.

"More or less," Mason replied. Most women Mason knew drowned their sorrows in chocolate or ice cream. But cheese? No doubt about it, Dana Preston was a most extraordinary woman.

Chapter Six

❦

Dana's battle with the chair had taught her one thing: if her shins—and most of Marion's belongings—were going to survive her stay, she needed a plan. So after mulling over possible options, Dana drove to the town grocery Tuesday morning and walked inside. "Could I speak to the manager, please?"

"Good morning, Dana!" came a voice from a nearby aisle. Dana turned to find Bart Salinas, Rita's husband from the Gingham Pocket B&B. "How are you liking Marion's place?"

Dana wasn't quite sure how to answer. "There sure is a lot of...decor in there."

Bart laughed. "There is indeed." He started unloading a full grocery cart of hot dogs, hamburgers, buns and condiments down onto the checkout counter. "Put this on the Busketeers' account, will you, Hannah?"

"God bless our Busketeers," replied the woman behind the counter.

Dana had to ask. "Busketeers?"

"You must be new in town," the woman replied. "Everybody in North Springs knows the Busketeers."

When Dana could only deliver a blank look, Bart explained. "Last year a bunch of us grandpa types from church decided we would get jobs driving the local school buses."

The woman began loading the items into a paper bag. "Bus-keteers, like Musketeers—get it?"

"But there are five of us," Bart added "Not three."

"That's pretty clever," Dana admired. "But I still don't get it."

Bart began putting the filled bags back into his cart. "Parents were saying kids were getting out of hand on the buses. Bullying, antics, that sort of thing. So the retirees' Bible study decided we'd take it on as a mission project of sorts. A way to be present for the young people in North Springs—without them figuring it out, of course."

The idea struck Dana as quirky and inventive and incredibly loving. She pictured a squad of grandfather-types waving kids onto buses in the morning, remembering their names and keeping an eye on the bullies who always seemed to lurk in the very back rows. "That's wonderful. Really."

"We try to be a force for good." He loaded another bag. "And a force for good needs funds. We're throwing a barbecue out at the gazebo tomorrow night. You should come. We grill a mean burger, us Busketeers."

Dana felt a smile cross her face at the thought. Here was exactly the sort of kindness she wanted to foster in the world. "I'm sure you do."

"Oh, don't let me keep you. You were looking for the manager, and here she is. Hannah, this is Dana Preston. She was staying with us for a few days before Rita arranged for her to rent Marion's place while she's up north with her son."

The woman extended her hand. "Hannah Young. Third Young to run the North Market. Welcome to North Springs." She waved as Bart made his way out the door. "Say hello to all the Busketeers for me!"

"Will do!" Bart called. "You coming tomorrow, Dana?"

"Maybe."

Hannah returned her gaze to Dana. "Great guys. They do way more than drive buses, but I expect you figured that out. Now, what can I do for you?"

Dana found she liked the woman's easy smile and friendly nature. "I'm finding Marion's house…" she searched for the right term, "…a bit treacherous. There's way too much to break. I figure I need to pack some of it up for safekeeping before I wreck anything." *Anything more*, she thought, remembering both the bruise on her shin and the busted chair. "I need about a half a dozen boxes. And some Bubble Wrap. And tape and markers."

Hannah's eyes lit with understanding rather than judgment. "Oh. Smart move. Must be hard to even turn around in that place. I'd be holding my breath every moment."

Dana was glad she felt free to laugh. "I need to give myself some maneuvering room—at least until she gets back."

Hannah smiled. "I like your plan. You bring your car or walk across the square?"

"My car's out front."

With a nod, Hannah began walking Dana toward the store entrance. "Bring it around back and I'll set you up good. Turn in the alley past the garden store and pull up in front of the red door. Give me five minutes."

Relieved, Dana replied, "Okay, thanks."

Have I really forgotten how nice people can be? Dana asked herself as she drove her car down behind the store and backed it up to face the Deliveries Only sign on the red door. A minute later, the door opened to reveal Hannah holding a stack of boxes nearly as high as she was.

Dana rushed to open the trunk of her car. "Wow, thanks."

"Got six more just inside. Duck in and help me, will you?"

Dana found the boxes, a stack of newspapers, and a brown paper bag with markers, masking tape and two rolls of Bubble Wrap. She picked them up and divided them between the trunk and the back seat of the car. If she was going to run a camp, she was going to need a truck or a Jeep or at least an SUV—but that was a problem for another day. Right now was about surviving Marion's house. Or, more precisely, about Marion's house surviving *her*. She turned back to Hannah, grateful. "What do I owe you for these?"

"Consider me the welcome wagon," Hannah said. "If you buy your groceries from me and not the big superstore out on the highway, I'll consider us even. Mind if I offer an idea?"

"Sure."

"I take it you've got a smartphone?"

Dana patted her jacket pocket. "Sure."

"Take photos of everything in its place before you pack it up. That way you can put it back just the way it was before Marion comes back. Not that she'd care if you moved it to keep it safe, but..." She raised an eyebrow at Dana.

"Great idea. I hadn't even gotten that far. I just felt like a bull in a china shop, you know?"

Hannah laughed. "I like you. Staying the whole summer?"

Frankly, it was looking like it might take that long to warm Mason Avery up to the idea. And she certainly wasn't in a hurry to return to Denver. Ever. Crawling back to Denver with her tail between her legs felt like the absolute last resort—she'd try everything before it came to that. "I think so."

"Let's get you set up with an account. I expect you need a few staples for your pantry?"

An account at the grocery store? People still did that sort of thing? "Actually, I do need groceries. And I did promise to buy them here."

Two bags of groceries and a heartening dose of friendly conversation later, Dana had all she needed for her next week at Marion's house.

"Bart and Rita are some of my favorite people," Hannah mentioned as she packed up the last of the groceries. "Our church would be sunk without folks like them. Have you been yet? To church?"

Dana searched for a safe way to answer that. "Rita mentioned it—a few dozen times."

Hannah laughed again. Some people laughed so easily. Had she ever been one of them? She couldn't remember…but she found she wanted to be. "That sounds like Rita. If you come—and I hope you do—come over and sit by me. If Bart doesn't grab you up to sit next to him and Rita first."

"Maybe I will." The ease of that statement caught Dana by surprise. It had to be at least ten years since she'd darkened the doors of a church for anything but a wedding or a funeral.

"Welcome to North Springs," Hannah called again as Dana squeezed the grocery bags into the last open spots in her car. "And be warned—lots of people who come to visit end up staying."

That's exactly what I have planned, Dana thought as she waved goodbye.

Mason couldn't just replace the leg on Marion's chair for Dana, it had been split too badly. It made him wonder how hard she'd fallen into it. Did he remember her having a bit of a limp at the diner, or was that just his imagination?

Truth was, his imagination was wandering a little too much in the direction of Dana Preston lately. He'd opted to go the extra mile for her and use a lathe to make a solid new replica of the old chair leg. He told himself it was a chance to practice one of his favorite parts of woodworking. But as he used the tool to slowly turn a square piece of wood into a rounded, curved chair leg, Dana's face—the curve of her cheekbone and the arch of her eyebrow—kept invading his thoughts.

He didn't realize how long he'd been giving the chair

a few final adjustments until Charlie got up from doing his school worksheets on his chair in the workshop and pronounced, "Can we just have dinner here? I don't wanna go down for hot dogs."

Charlie? Turn down hot dogs? Mason could hardly believe his ears. "What do you mean, you don't want to go?"

Charlie just stared at the sawdust on the shop floor. "I don't wanna go."

"You've been bugging me to go all week. I bought tickets and everything. I think we should go. And we need to bring Miss Dana her chair back, remember? It's ready to put in the truck and go."

"No." His son gave the single word an impressive amount of finality. Some days Mason had to wonder who really was in charge here. It took so much energy to manage Charlie lately—energy he couldn't seem to find. Nothing was easy with his son anymore.

Mason tried again. "This isn't about what happened at school, is it? You have friends at school, and everybody makes mistakes. It'll be fine."

Charlie's lower lip stuck out. "I see those kids all week. I see 'em on the bus. I see 'em everywhere."

Mason wasn't sure he agreed. Mrs. Booker had confirmed Mason's worries that Charlie wasn't interacting with other kids at school enough. He was teaching his son to be too much of a loner—by poor example, if he was honest. Charlie did have one or two friends, which probably wasn't enough for a boy his age. He rarely went anywhere after school. He should be in Little League, or spending Saturdays playing with friends.

Instead, Charlie rarely seemed eager to venture beyond the fences of home. "You sure everything's okay? At school, I mean?"

"Yup." The way Charlie said it, it sounded much more like "Not really."

Mason sat down on the chair and pulled Charlie into his lap. "Let's see if we can guess who'll be there." He racked his brain for the names of Charlie's schoolmates other than the one whose Mom had berated him for the window incident. "Taylor? Will he be there, you think?"

"Maybe." Evidently Taylor's presence wasn't much of an incentive.

"What about Scotty? His mom's involved in all that kind of stuff."

"Probably." Again, no sign of any real enthusiasm.

Finally, a possible reason for Charlie's reluctance dawned on Mason. "Are you worried Willy will be there? Or Nathan?"

Charlie's sunken shoulders told Mason he'd hit on the real problem.

Truth be told, Mason had also been tempted to skip the Busketeers barbecue fundraiser despite the promise of good food. Still, Dana's words about needing to push himself back into the world had been eating at him. This self-imposed isolation was easier, but it wasn't good for Charlie.

Melony was always the one to get involved in stuff like this, making friends easily even though Mason's family had been in the area for three generations. "I still think we should go. And we can leave right after we eat if you don't want to stay. And tell you what," he added in a burst of inspiration, "how about we stop by the hobby store on the way? Get you something new to build."

That was the ticket. Charlie straightened up so fast Mason wondered why it hadn't occurred to him to suggest this in the first place. "A boat this time?"

"Could be."

Mason pulled off his work apron and took Charlie's hand to walk back toward the house. *I'm trying, Melony. I'll do all I can to make it okay for him.*

As they piled themselves and Marion's chair into the truck, Charlie hesitated. "Will Mr. Bart be there?"

"Your bus driver, Mr. Salinas?" Maybe Charlie hadn't worked out that the Busketeer bus drivers were running the thing this year. "Sure. All the Busketeers are cooking."

Charlie's face fell. "Oh."

"I thought you liked him. You said he was nice."

"He was."

"He isn't anymore?" That didn't seem like Bart Salinas. The guy was one of the nicest people in North Springs. He'd been wonderful to Charlie since the accident. Mason considered it a particular blessing that he'd been the driver assigned to Charlie's route.

"He got mad at me yesterday."

That really didn't sound like Bart Salinas. "Why?"

"Well, he really got mad at Willy. But sorta me, too, I think."

Charlie had seemed a little off when he got home yesterday afternoon. "Why did Mr. Bart get mad at Willy?" That seemed a safer question.

"Dunno."

Mason watched Charlie's expression in the rearview mirror. He wasn't so old that he didn't remember giving that same answer to his own father when what he really meant was "I don't wanna tell you."

"Take a guess. Willy must have done something." Mason started the truck, hoping it sent the message, "We're going anyway, so you might as well tell me before Mr. Bart does."

After about a full minute of sulking silence, Charlie mumbled, "Doug was being an idiot."

"To Willy?" After a moment he thought to add, "To you?"

"To everybody. Willy told him off."

Now the picture was getting a little clearer. As they paused at a stop sign with no one else around, Mason turned to face Charlie for a moment. "Just told him off?" He raised an eyebrow at his son to let him know he wanted a straight answer. After all, wasn't it Willy who suggested being mean right back?

Charlie shrunk back against the seat. "Doug fell out of the seat. By himself. Willy hardly even pushed him. 'Cuz Doug is a jerk."

"Okay, things like this are why I'm not sure Willy is a good friend."

Oh, that wasn't the smartest thing to say. Dana was right—Mason could practically watch the defiance jut Charlie's chin out farther.

"It's important to learn to get along with people." Mason's brain pulled up an image of the look Dana Preston might give him for a platitude like that. "Everybody has to try and do that," he added with a tinge of guilt. "Now let's go get us a good hot dog."

As he parked his truck along the square and tried to ignore the knot in his gut at being among all the friendly people, Mason told himself that everybody *did* have to try.

Including him.

Chapter Seven

"Bart told me he'd invited you!" Rita called out the minute she caught sight of Dana walking across the square toward the gazebo on Wednesday evening. "I can't believe I didn't think of it."

Dana had talked herself out of coming twice since Bart's invitation. Still, she didn't have much right to lecture Mason on staying isolated if she did the same herself. He said he was meeting her at Marion's house later, but that didn't stop Dana from looking for him and Charlie among the rows of tables and tablecloths in circles around the gazebo.

"It's Busketeer Barbecue night. Used to just be a school thing, but since Bart and the Busketeers took the whole thing over, everybody just calls it the Busketeer Barbecue." Rita tucked Dana's arm into her elbow and began leading her toward the crowd. "They've gone overboard on the Busketeers thing if you ask me, but you cannot tell that man *nada* when he gets a thought into that head of his."

"Someone once said that of me," Dana offered. Only Captain Derrick hadn't said it with the begrudging, loving tolerance in Rita's tone. She wondered what the captain would say if she told him what she was up to now?

Rita stopped and gave Dana a look. "I expect that's true. You have spine. Drive. World needs more of that, if you ask me." Her eyes brightened as she waved to someone. "Oh, look, there's Martha Booker, from the school."

Dana didn't know whether to say how she knew the teacher. Had Mason told anyone about the rock incident? The whole thing still worried her deeply.

"You'd like Martha. And Bart told me you've met Hannah. Seems to me like you two will end up being friends—you're about the same age." Rita's face suddenly lost its sparkle. "And there's Arthur Nicholson. If you want to talk about the difference between good stubborn and bad stubborn, he's it."

Dana had seen that name on several of the forms that needed to be submitted for the camp. That didn't bode well. It wasn't hard to size up the man by the way he walked—more of a strut, actually. "Why?"

"Arthur has his own opinions of how things ought to be done around here. He makes sure we all know when we fall short of his big fat measuring stick. He thinks the Busketeers are silly, mostly because he can't imagine North Springs having any kind of problems. Steer clear of that one."

Dana wasn't going to have that luxury. Still, she turned to Rita. "The Busketeers aren't silly. Do you know how many kids I've seen who might have headed down a different path if they knew at least one adult was pulling for them? Even just the smallest bit?" Dana watched Arthur Nicholson walk up to the gazebo as if it were a monument to his importance. It would have been nobler not to take such an instant dislike to the man, but her instincts rarely misled her. "No sir, the Busketeers are brilliant. The world needs a whole bunch more Busketeers if you ask me."

Rita touched Dana's arm, and Dana noticed the woman's eyes well up a bit. "You make sure Bart hears you say that. Some days that man needs a little reminder just how wonderful he is. And he certainly isn't going to get it from Arthur."

"Count on it." Dana made a mental note to herself to catch Bart and offer up some praise for what he and the other Busketeers were doing. Something like that could matter so much to a kid that age.

As for Arthur Nicholson, he seemed like the kind of obstacle best met head-on. She had best start getting on his good side to do what she wanted to do. "Would you introduce me to Arthur?" she asked Rita.

"Well, aren't you a brave one," Rita declared.

"Might as well start making all the friends I can," Dana said to Rita's look of surprise. It felt a bit silly, but she wasn't ready to admit to Rita why she needed Nicholson's endorsement. "Maybe I'll discover his good side."

"I'm pretty sure it went missing years ago. But hope springs eternal. Come on." Rita briskly walked up to the gazebo steps where Arthur seemed to be holding court as people lined up to get their dinners from the crew of cooking Busketeers.

"Arthur," Rita began in a voice so sweet Dana couldn't help but grin. "I'd like you to meet Miss Preston. Dana's thinking about moving here. She's staying in Marion's place until we all can convince her to unpack her bags for good."

Arthur extended a hand. "North Springs is a wonderful place to call home. I'm sure Rita hasn't lost an opportunity to tell you that."

Dana managed a small laugh. "If she isn't on your tourism council, she ought to be."

"People are proud of North Springs." He gestured around the square and the people gathered at tables sharing food. "Not many places like this around anymore."

"It is a special place, I'll give you that." Dana was startled how special it already seemed to be to her.

"See," Rita cooed. "We got her already. Never takes much, does it, Arthur?"

"It takes protecting and planning and commitment to keep it that way. Solid communities take nurturing."

Dana could have done without the private speech on the subject, but she nodded in agreement with Nicholson. It wasn't the concept that bugged her as much as his attitude that he seemed to be the only one in possession of *how* protecting and planning and commitment ought to be done.

Rita seemed done with it, too. "Well, tonight it takes Busketeers and hot dogs. Such a fun event, don't you think? Smells delicious. Those men can sure cook up a storm."

"I'll go up and get mine in a minute. I've got a few more people to say hello to," Arthur replied, casting his eyes over Dana's shoulder before walking away.

"Is he mayor?"

"Oh, no, hon. But you can't tell him that. Officially, he chairs the zoning commission. Unofficially, he thinks he runs the place." Rita gave a small grunt. "A sort of self-appointed watchdog. And not a very nice one at that."

Mason caught up with Dana just after she left the hot dog line. He'd watched her interaction with Arthur Nicholson from a distance as he and Charlie were getting their own food. What happened didn't surprise him in the slightest: Nicholson dismissed her as unimportant.

That bothered him more than it should have. Dana—not just her idea but the woman herself—was getting under his skin. He was actually starting to *want* this to work.

Just how did that happen? Crazy, pie-in-the-sky ideas like this camp of hers were not in his nature. Then again, did he even have a nature anymore? Something long cold and empty seemed to be breaking open in him, and he was running out of ways to ignore that it was Dana making it happen. To call the whole thing uncomfortable was an understatement—but at least it was something that could be classified as a feeling.

He saw the set of Dana's shoulders as Nicholson found someone else more worthy of his attention. *You'll regret that*, he warned Arthur in his mind. *She's feisty.*

As Mason helped Charlie open his bag of potato chips, he ignored the irrational zing that went through him as Dana caught his eye over the festive crowd. She was glad to see him. It was because Arthur was being Arthur, he told himself. Nobody left that man's presence feeling better about themselves but Arthur. And maybe the small circle of Arthur's friends who were so sure they knew what was best for North Springs. He rarely agreed with Arthur on civic matters, and Mason had the feeling that would happen again regarding Dana's camp.

"Hi, Miss Dana," Charlie called with his mouth full of potato chips. "Didya get a hot dog already?" Mason was glad to hear some enthusiasm for the event finally show up in Charlie's tone. Was it the event? Or the woman in front of him? The remarkable connection his son seemed to have with Dana—and she with him—continued to baffle him.

"Just a minute ago," she said, making a show of patting her stomach as she came over and took a seat across the table from Mason and Charlie. "Those Busketeers are good cooks."

"I see you met Arthur Nicholson," Mason offered.

Her lips thinned to a near frown. "I did."

"He's the biggest challenge you'll face to get this thing off the ground."

The frown disappeared, replaced by the hint of a smile Mason found he liked very much. "I thought that was you."

"*Next* to me," he corrected. "Even if I say yes, Arthur can still say no. And saying no is one of Arthur's specialties."

They both turned to watch Arthur talking among some rather pretentious-looking residents. "Rita was right," Dana said warily. "He does look as if he runs the place."

"I'm surprised he didn't tell you that himself. He'll insist you get his approval. And, unfortunately, as chair of the zoning committee, he's right."

She planted her elbows on the table. "I did see his name on lots of those town forms."

Charlie looked up at Dana. "Are you really gonna make a summer camp?"

Dana looked at Mason with a *how do you want me to answer that?* expression.

"She's thinking up ideas," Mason answered for her. "There are lots of things to work out before we decide if it makes sense."

"Why? Who wouldn't want a summer camp near our house?" Charlie seemed to think this was a great idea. Mason had been deliberately vague in his explanation of things that Charlie hadn't quite caught on to the fact that the camp would *be* their property, not just near it. "Will it have a swimming pool?"

Dana laughed. He hadn't heard her laugh yet. She had a nice laugh. Gentle and surprisingly musical for so practical a woman. "We haven't gotten that far."

There she was, using "we" again. Arthur Nicholson had better get ready for the fight of his life. That was, if Mason gave the go-ahead. The possibility was looking stronger all the time, but none of that would matter if the zoning board nixed it, and Mason was pretty sure they would.

That ought to have felt safe, but instead it just felt sad. There was a growing part of him that didn't want to hand Dana that kind of disappointment.

Dana rose. "Well, you two enjoy your dinner and come on over to the house with the chair when you're done." She gave Charlie the warmest of smiles. "I just might have a few cookies for a certain someone when you do."

That got Charlie's attention. "Dad, can we go right now?"

Mason found himself laughing. The strange sensation didn't feel as foreign as he expected. "How about we make a try at a decent dinner before cookies?" Of course, hot dogs, chips and watermelon might not qualify as a decent dinner to some, but the fact that they were eating down among everyone at town made up for any nutritional weakness.

"See you soon?" Dana said.

Decent dinner or not, Mason found he shared Charlie's desire to get up and follow Dana right there and then.

Which is exactly why he told himself to stay put and eat.

It didn't make any sense that she was nervous.

Sure, the house was an oddball collection of knick-knacks that would drive most people to distraction, but it wasn't her house. Mason wouldn't consider the over-the-top decorating—even now that she'd packed half of it away for sheer personal safety—to be a reflection of her taste.

Dana combed her fingers through her hair again and fought the thought that refused to go away: she wanted him to like her.

For professional reasons, she told herself in the mirror over the fireplace—now that she could actually see her reflection with the two dozen chubby porcelain angels who had previously crowded the mantel boxed away. Mason needed to see her as a pleasant and effective business partner. Someone with a strong vision and solid plans. She had to be more than just a signature on a check to him if this was ever going to work. Mason wasn't the kind of man to entrust his family land to just any buyer.

And besides, she wasn't looking for a seller. She was looking for a *partner*. A *business* partner.

Yes, it was for a visionary idea—a cause, really—but it wouldn't seem to stay just that. The original urge that "only this land will do" was fast transforming into "only this man and his land."

"Only this man and his boy and his land," if she were being totally honest.

That total honesty scared her to death. She'd sat in that quirky little diner having lunch with Mason Avery and liking it. A lot. She'd sought him out to regain her moorings after Arthur Nicholson looked down his nose at her. She'd teased him and enjoyed hearing his resulting laughter. All of those reasons that had very little to do with Camp True North Springs.

That's what it was called now, Camp True North Springs.

The name had come to her on the walk home from

the square as she looked north to the one tallest mountain you could see from anywhere in North Springs. She'd never been especially great with directions, but the one thing she liked about North Springs was that you could look up, find that one plateau and figure out where you were. True North was an anchor, a guiding force, a way to chart your course. That's what the camp would be. It had literally stopped her steps on the sidewalk, landing in her chest with the same power the idea had in the first place. She hadn't planned to name it— not yet—but it was as if she no longer had any choice.

Was she worried that he wouldn't like the name? she asked herself. After all, her hands had almost shook as she swapped out her old file folder with a new one freshly inked with the name. *You know that's not the reason.* Her police-trained radar for falsehoods was doing her no favors tonight. If no one ever pulled the wool over Detective Dana Preston's eyes, why should her own self be any different?

Chapter Eight

$\sim$

Marion's doorbell, it turned out, was as supremely fussy as the woman's decor. Dana cringed when the device chimed out "Fly Me to the Moon," in calliope tones. She could hear Mason laughing on the other side of the door as she pulled it open.

"I didn't know it did that!" she admitted, feeling embarrassed for no real reason. "Marion was always at the door when I arrived."

"I suppose I should have—*whoa*." Mason stopped as he caught sight of the multiple menageries still behind her. "Charlie, keep your hands in your pockets and walk slow."

Charlie peered into the room. "Can we come in and see the lady's house full of silly things?"

Mason's face paled. "I *did not* say her things were silly," he retorted with a horrified look. "I said she had a lot of things that shouldn't be touched in her house."

"Isn't that the same thing?" The boy scratched one ear like a lost dog. "That's sure a silly doorbell."

"It's different," Dana had to agree. "And you are going to have to watch where you walk. Can you promise me you'll be extra careful? It's bad enough I've already broken Mrs. Gilbert's chair."

As if to declare his cooperation, Charlie made a show of stuffing both hands resolutely in his pockets.

Despite the young-bull-in-a-china-shop threat, Dana was glad Charlie was here. It made the whole situation easier, made the visit less about her and Mason—which was absurd, because the visit wasn't ever about her and Mason, right?

"I'll take Charlie straight to the kitchen," she suggested to Mason's worried expression. "There's less of—well, less of everything there and I have some lemonade to go along with those cookies."

"How about I bring the chair in through the side door?" Mason replied, giving the still-stuffed room a once-over. "Less to navigate that way."

Mason turned back toward the truck and Dana turned toward the kitchen. For whatever reason, she held out a hand to Charlie. Maybe because she remembered feeling as if she needed a guide through the overstuffed house on her first visit, too.

Charlie stared at his hand, still sunk into his pocket and back to her open palm.

"It's okay," she said with a chuckle of understanding. "I'll get you there safely."

"There's a million things in here," Charlie said. His eyes were wide in a sort of dumbfounded awe. She supposed the whole place looked like a prissy museum to a boy of his age.

"A lot of them are already packed away," Dana admitted. "There used to be a gazillion."

Charlie laughed, slid his hand from his pocket and slipped it into hers. The simple act of trust sunk deep under her skin.

His steps slowed as they passed a flock of peacocks packed onto a lamp stand table, their tails in various stages of closed to opened in a full colorful display. "I kept those out 'cause I kinda like 'em," she said. "Whatd'ya think?"

"There's too many of 'em," Charlie said. He wheeled his head around. "There's too many of *everything*."

That was a pretty fair description of Marion's home. She didn't blame the boy when he exhaled upon making it safely to the kitchen. Still, there had to be at least twelve cookie jars crowding the counters. "Are all those full?" he asked hopefully.

"That would be fun, wouldn't it?" Dana reached into a cabinet and pulled out a box of ordinary sugar cookies. "I've only got these, but they should be nice with lemonade." A woman handing out lemonade and cookies. No one she recognized in herself, that's for sure.

"So you live here?" Charlie looked as startled at the idea as she'd just felt.

"No, I'm just staying for a while," until she found her own place, she added silently. "Oh, here's your dad."

Mason had appeared with the chair at the side door just off the kitchen. "Made it safely?" he asked as he angled himself and the chair through the narrow door.

"We did." Dana pointed to the empty spot by the kitchen table.

Mason set the chair down, then peered back through the archway where she and Charlie had just come. "I'd heard people talk about it, but I never…" He shrugged. "You say half of it's packed away?" He looked again, then looked back at her. "Seriously?"

"You get used to it." Dana wasn't sure she believed it, but it sounded like the kind of thing to say.

Charlie settled himself on one of the chairs, making Dana realize she'd set the stage for a visit, not just dropping off a chair. It felt rather nice, to have friends come over for a visit. "Lemonade?" That felt wildly out of character the minute she said it, but Charlie nodded and Mason sat down.

"All those cookie jars and no cookies," Charlie murmured.

When Mason scowled at his son's frank observation, Dana added, "Well, just store-bought ones. I'm not much of a baker. In fact, I'm not a baker at all."

"I never met a cookie I didn't like," Mason offered with a smile.

"Me neither!" Charlie looked so much like his father just then that Dana felt a moment of ache in her heart. People always remarked about how much she looked like her own father. Pop was a terrific father, and while he never said it openly, she knew he pined for the chance to be a terrific grandfather. Not everybody gets what they want.

Mason picked up the hymnal from where Dana had forgotten it was still lying open on the table. "Church? I haven't seen you there yet, have I?"

Dana felt her face flush. "Oh, that's Marion's. I was

just…" She couldn't possibly reveal to him what she'd been doing Sunday night with the hymnal. "…looking through it. Seeing what I remembered from my younger days." She held out her hand to accept the tattered volume from Mason, and their fingers touched as he handed it off. Dana tried to dismiss the startling sparkle that hummed under her skin where they'd touched. This was definitely not the time or place for any sort of attraction to that man. If she had to make a list of things that would jeopardize the partnership she was trying to establish, getting involved would take the top spot.

The barbecue—where Arthur had so deftly put Dana in her place—was the first time Mason had ever seen Dana falter. Usually the woman radiated confidence and purpose. And yet she'd looked skittish after her conversation with Arthur, and even more off-balance and wary now. Mason supposed he could put it down to trying to live in this china shop of a house, but that wasn't it. There was something else, something he could sense but couldn't quite name.

The open hymnal was a surprise. He regretted picking it up in an effort to make conversation—it seemed to embarrass her that he'd noticed it.

"What's True North Springs?" Charlie asked, pointing to the handwritten label on a thick file—a brand new one—on the table.

If Dana had flushed at the hymnal, she went pale at Charlie's question.

Charlie's eyebrows scrunched up in thought. "Do we live in a fake North Springs?"

"No," Dana replied right away, her tone rushed and breathless. She pulled the file toward her, angling the label away from Mason as if she could hide it. "It's… well…it's the name that came to me for the camp."

She'd named the camp? Wasn't that really getting ahead of herself?

"Why'd you pick that name?" Charlie asked the question as if it had a simple answer. Mason didn't expect that was the case at all. True North. Wasn't it what everyone was searching for? What seemed to have been stripped from his life in these past years? The power of the name—to anyone but most especially to him— sunk into his being in a way that both pulled him in and pushed him away at the same time.

It took her a moment to find the words to answer. In those seconds, Mason saw a glimpse of the woman Dana most likely hid from the world. Tender in a way he hadn't expected. Vulnerable. Wounded, even, despite her insistence that she was healing. After all, he, more than most people, knew that healing wasn't the same thing as having a wound go away. Some wounds heal over, but they're always there. The thought took the spark of connection he felt to Dana and gave it new power.

"Well, there's the North Springs connection, obviously. And it doesn't mean the town is fake—not at all. Some grown-ups talk about something called 'true north.' A way you're sure of, something that doesn't change." She kept looking down, as if it was hard to hold Charlie's gaze or even his own. But when she did catch his eye, even for a moment, there was a fire of purpose in her eyes. "It's a way to find your path home—or, I suppose, the path to where you need to be. It's a guiding force."

She saw the camp as a true north. For the kids, and probably even for her. What about him? Could taking the land he'd thought was his grounding point and turning it into the true north for others be his own true north as well? The thought spun in his head with a tangle of ideas.

"Like God?" Charlie asked. He clearly liked the idea. That tucked itself into a warm corner of Mason's heart. His one hope for his son was that he'd come out of this whole mess still believing the world was a good place and that God loved him. Some days he was more confident of that than others.

Dana let out an unsteady breath. "Some people might say it's God. Not everyone, I guess. Lots of people believe God guides them. Maybe they just have to start with the idea of a true north, and then they can learn about how God is that for people."

Dana looked as if she were trying the concept on for size. Pastor Gorman had talked about the sacred moments where God began His journey into people's lives, where they woke up to the idea that God cared about them and what they faced. Mason couldn't shake the notion that he was seeing just that. It did that thing again to his sense of connection to Dana. He'd thought of her as always pushing toward him—it rattled him to think of himself as being pulled toward her.

"Do you?" Charlie asked. *Ah, kids*, Mason thought.

They could nail you to the wall with a single question without even realizing what they're doing.

Even though he found himself wanting to know the answer, Mason gave Dana an out by saying, "That's not the kind of question you ask just anybody."

Charlie's resulting look roughly translated to "Sure seems that way to me."

"No," Dana cut in, "it's okay. It's a fair question." She shifted in her chair. "Do I? Well, I used to be a whole lot more sure when I was your age. At my job I saw people go the wrongest way there is. But I've seen God guide other people, I know that." She laid a hand across the thick file, as if the answer would come to her from within the stack of papers. "I had some things happen to me. Bad things. And I think that's making it hard for me to see the guiding. So I guess I can't quite figure out my true north yet. And I think there are people—kids especially—who feel like me. That's why the camp is so important to me."

Mason watched how Charlie would respond to so frank an answer from an adult. He rather liked that Dana didn't just feed Charlie a pretty speech or an easy answer. She was doing Charlie the honor of giving him the truth—or at least her truth. He respected that.

"Me, too," Charlie said with a simple nod. "I can't figure it out much some days."

A warmth spread over Dana's face. "Maybe like the day you threw that rock? 'Cause you couldn't figure out what else to do?"

Charlie's eyes dropped to the table. "Sorta." A pang of sorrow jabbed into Mason's heart. *I feel like that so much. Like I can't figure out what else to do.* Dana was right—he needed to straighten his own path, shore up his own journey, so that he could truly help his son.

The trouble was that it seemed like God had laid a path out right in front of him—*literally* right in front of him at the moment—but he couldn't bring himself to take it.

The name on the file folder label seemed to be calling to him, compelling him as much as the bravery in Dana's eyes. If he stayed much longer, he might say yes to something he had no business saying yes to just yet. This enormous leap wasn't anything to take lightly. It would change his and Charlie's life forever.

"We'll just have a couple of cookies and some lemonade, Charlie. Then we should get going." If he stayed too long, Mason feared he might let his loneliness make this decision for him. *That land is Charlie's future. Camp True North Springs could fail. There's no walking away from it if that happens. You owe Charlie that land, that heritage. What do you owe her?* Dana had only the beginnings of a plan. She had only scraps of faith, if that. She had emotional baggage and physical wounds.

And yet she had something that stirred a deep connection in him, whether he wanted to admit it or not.

Dana turned her gaze to him, and the zing he'd been trying to ignore grew to a hum he seemed to feel everywhere. There was a moment—both heavy and light at the same time—before she asked, "What do I owe you?"

Mason stared at her, worried his thoughts had somehow come out aloud. "Huh?"

"The chair? What do I owe you for the repairs?"

"Nothing," he said without thinking. "You helped Charlie and I the other night." Mason didn't know how he would have gotten through that episode without her help. That was at least worth some lumber, half an hour of his time and half a pint of wood stain. But he couldn't let it buy his full cooperation on the camp. At least not yet.

Just as he was going out the door, as Charlie was already on his way to the truck, Dana caught his elbow. The touch startled him, but the way she leaned in startled him even more. She drew her face close enough that he could smell the scent of whatever it was she used on her hair. It wasn't fussy or floral, and he liked the way it suited her. "Have you figured out what to do about the pond yet?" she whispered.

There wasn't a worse question she could have asked—it jabbed right to the heart of all he was feeling lately. "No," he gulped out, feeling raw and open at the admission. How could he make a pond reappear out of thin air? The wide area of cracked earth that once was Melony's favorite spot on the property seemed all too fitting a metaphor for his life lately. Dry, lifeless and not at all what it needed to be for Charlie. He'd been praying for a solution, but nothing had come to him.

And time was running out.

"You'll think of something," she said, but neither of them fully believed the assurance.

He could only offer a doubtful shrug. Friday was a mere two days away. "I'd better. I'm running out of time."

Chapter Nine

This feels so normal.

It was an odd reaction to walking around the square with Hannah Young Thursday morning, but when the friendly neighborhood grocer—as Hannah liked to call herself—had invited her out for coffee, Dana was pleased to accept. Hannah was easy and generous with her friendship. So easy, in fact, that Dana had opened up just the tiniest bit about her plans. Nothing too specific, nothing to tie it to Mason Avery or his property, just the nugget of the idea.

Hannah connected the vision to Charlie without any encouragement from Dana. "Poor little guy, I wish there was something like that for him. In fact, I can think of three families who are reeling from some kind of violence. Who wouldn't want to give those souls a breath of fresh air—literally?"

Dana smiled at the encouragement until Hannah's own smile dissolved. "Well, there's the answer to my question," she grumbled, nodding in the direction of Arthur

Nicholson. The man was coming down the steps of the town hall that sat in the center of the square. "I expect you already know it will take a lot of convincing to get him to go for something like that around here."

While she'd never been one to kiss up to bureaucrats, Dana would do whatever it took to bring Arthur around. "He's a tough nut to crack, I admit. But I'm trying. I figure if I can talk a kid off a window ledge—and I have, twice—I can coax a guy like him into saying yes."

"That's the spirit," Hannah teased as they walked past the garden store. "Oh, will you look at that? How sweet!"

Dana turned to see a little miniature water feature set up in the window of the store. The concrete tub had stylized metal plants around it, complete with lily pads and an adorable clay frog that spit water out into the pond.

A pond.

Dana's steps froze.

Charlie needed a pond. And not just any pond, his own pond, according to Mason. Couldn't this be Charlie's pond for tomorrow?

"Could we go inside?" Dana asked, trying not to show the instant sense of urgency she felt.

Hannah pulled the door open with a quizzical look. "You want a pond? Doesn't Marion have something like six birdbaths?"

"It's not for me. It's for Charlie Avery."

Dana ignored the quizzical look on Hannah's face as she walked past the grocer into the store. "It's a long story."

"I expect it is. And I'm gonna want to hear it. Hey,

Mike," she called to the man behind the counter, "You want to come sell Dana here the pond in your window?"

Mike, a friendly-looking man with a mop of black hair and bright eyes, settled some seed packets on the shelf behind him and walked up to Dana. "In the market for a water feature?" he asked.

Dana was pulling in a breath to give something close to a reasonable answer when Hannah cut in. "She wants to buy this because, for some reason she's about to explain to us, Charlie Avery needs a pond."

The small-town stereotype of everybody needing to know everything about everybody else seemed to be playing out right in front of her eyes. "Um, yes," she said, still trying to figure out how to start the explanation.

Mike walked toward the window with them. "Kind of an expensive gift for someone Charlie's age. This isn't a toy. I've got some wading pools out back if you're looking for that sort of thing."

"No, it has to be a pond. By tomorrow." Dana took a deep breath and gave the best explanation she could about Melony Avery's Hawaiian heritage and the tradition she'd had. "Their pond dried up. And he's upset he can't keep up the tradition."

"So this little thing will stand in for the pond that's dried up on Avery's land, huh?"

When Mike said it out loud, it sounded ridiculous. What was she thinking, poking her nose into Mason's family history like that, dreaming up a lame excuse for an important family memory? Dana was losing perspective when it came to Mason and Charlie, letting her emotions run away with her good cop sense. "It's probably a dumb idea," she confessed, wishing she'd never come into the store. Where was this impulsive nature coming from? These wild ideas pulling her down strange paths?

"I don't think it's dumb at all," Mike said. "I wish I'd known. Poor kid's been through so much. The drought's been affecting us all, but something like that? Well, seems a shame." He leaned in. "And seems he's had a real go of it lately." By way of explanation, he added, "Martha Booker, his teacher, is my aunt. She's worried about the boy. So no, I don't think it's a silly gesture at all. Shows real heart, if you ask me." He picked up the ceramic frog and began detaching it from the water tube. "Tell you what. I'll give you the whole setup for ten dollars."

For the first time it occurred to Dana that she might have been wise to look at the price tag for the set before storming in here declaring her intentions to buy it for Charlie. A quick glance showed he'd priced the set at $150. "You can't give that to me for ten dollars."

Mike smiled. "I can. And I will."

"No, you won't," cut in Hannah, "Because I'm going to give you ten as well. And I'll get Rita and Bart to pitch in ten each as well, so you'll get forty—which still isn't enough." She looked at Dana. "We've all been sitting around wishing there was something we could do for Mason and Charlie, and you swoop into town and figure out how to actually do something. Good for you."

Mike was already heading to the back of the shop

for a box. "So you need flowers, you say?" he called over his shoulder as he pulled the container off a shelf.

"I think so."

"Does it have to be a—what's that fancy Hawaiian name for it? A lei?" He put the box on the counter, deposited the frog in one corner and then headed to the window for the large dish that made up the pond.

Dana searched her memory of Mason's explanation. "No, just some flowers." What if they had to be a certain kind of flowers? Melony's favorite color or something? How could she think this dinky stand-in would make things okay for Charlie? "At least I think so."

Mike dumped the existing water out of the decorative tub and settled it into the box. Hannah was already coming back from the window with the small motorized pump. "Here," she said, handing the device to Dana. "Hold this while I make a call."

Dana took the pump and handed it to Mike. The sense of being caught up in something bigger than herself surged up over her again, raising a lump in her throat. "You all don't have to…"

Hannah held up a stern finger to hush her while she dialed her cell phone. "Lorna," she said when the person on the other end picked up the call, "can you donate a delivery of a small bunch of pretty flowers to Mason Avery's place tomorrow? A few of us are putting together a little…something for Charlie. Something Melony used to do for him." Hannah nodded and gave a thumbs-up. "Color?" she asked Dana.

"I don't know," Dana said, feeling a strange combination of excited and off-balance. The feeling had been her nearly daily companion since coming to North Springs.

"Melony colors. Could you make a guess? Thanks, hon." Hannah ended the call as if she'd done nothing more ordinary than order a pizza. "Pond, water, frog, flowers. Anything else?"

Dana reached for her handbag. "No. You've done more than enough as it is."

Mike pushed his palm toward Dana. "Actually, I don't think I can take any money for this. Mason's been a good customer. And little Charlie…" He shook his head. "Put that money away."

"But I should—" Dana sputtered.

"You came in and told me about a need and had the idea how to meet it. That's worth way more than your money any day of the week. I'm kind of sorry it took a newcomer to do what we all ought to have done."

"Dana's looking to move here," Hannah offered. "She's staying in Marion's place until she can find a spot of her own."

"Marion's?" Mike's eyes widened with the same surprise everyone had when they discovered she was staying in Marion Gilbert's house. If Dana had realized the high-profile status staying amidst the woman's myriad of collections would have given her, she might have kept her room at the Gingham Pocket. "I've only been in there once to deliver a birdbath and…well, you are a brave soul."

"It's not that bad," Dana said. "I just have to be careful."

Mike tucked the last of the ornamental grass in around the tub. "Will you come back in and let me know how it all goes? Such a sad thing, that was. I keep waiting for Mason to surface, but it doesn't seem like he has. All up there by himself on the mountain. Seems a lonely life. I'll say a prayer this helps."

"I don't see how it can do anything but help," Hannah added. "It's a brilliant idea."

"Thanks," Dana said to the both of them, truly meaning it. "I kept hoping there was something—" she started to say "I could do," but edited it to "—to be done." She no longer felt in control of how personal her connection to Mason and Charlie had become. That was a bad thing, right? Wildly uncomfortable, yes, but she couldn't quite bring herself to see it as bad. The sheer ability to feel— even that—had been missing from her life for too long.

"Well, thanks to you, now there is." Mike hoisted the box with the kindest of smiles. "Where are you parked? I'll get you loaded up and on your way."

Help me, Lord. There's got to be something I can do to make this better.

Mason was standing in his workshop late Thursday afternoon, staring out the window at the circle of caked earth that used to be a pond. Staring at the pretty little bench he'd built for Melony on the near side, under the slice of shade offered by a nearby tree. The empty bench, the one he could only bring himself to sit on when Charlie asked to go there. Even then, it took all his energy to mask the pain and hope he was making a way for Charlie to build a new set of memories in the special spot.

A tug on his work apron dragged him from his thoughts. "Dad!" Charlie had gotten up from the little corner of the workshop where he often did his home-work while Mason worked. *"Dad!"* he repeated louder, practically yanking on the apron now. "Where are your listening ears?"

It was a saying his teacher used often. "Sorry, kiddo. I was trying to figure something out."

He was glad Charlie assumed it was something about the hinges he was fastening to a cabinet. "The gate's buzzing," Charlie said impatiently. "Don't you hear it?"

In fact, the intercom speaker for the front gate in the workshop was indeed going off. How had he been so lost in thought that he'd not heard the signal? He walked over and pressed the button. "Hello?"

"It's Dana. I…um… I have something for you. For Charlie, actually. Could I drop it off?"

Again, he noticed the new unsteadiness in her voice. She was different than the usual bulldozer of confidence she'd been earlier. Or was he just imagining it? Letting his unwelcome fascination for her play tricks on his ears?

Charlie looked up at him with an expectant grin. Of course, now that she'd mentioned whatever she brought was for Charlie, he couldn't hope to refuse. But before he had the chance, Charlie reached up and pressed the button to shout, "Sure!"

He didn't really mean the scowl he sent his son. Charlie wasn't supposed to answer or use the intercom without permission, but who could blame the boy for wanting whatever gift was coming his way? Especially with tomorrow looming the way it was? "Of course," he said, pressing the button that unlocked the gate. "We're in the shop."

Charlie raced out the door to watch for Dana's car to come up the drive. Mason took a deep breath, hung up his leather work apron and dusted the worst of the sawdust off his hands and clothes.

Dana got out of the car and waved to Charlie. Something about the half eager, half sheepish expression on her face sunk deep into him. "Hi, Miss Dana!" Charlie shouted, waving back. "Whatcha got? Whatcha got?"

"Well," Dana replied, looking from Charlie to Mason. "It's sort of a solution, I hope. Not just me, actually." She shrugged, walking around to the trunk of her car. "Hannah from the grocery and Mike from the garden store pitched in. I hope you don't mind. Really."

Babbling? From Dana Preston? Mason walked closer, unable to guess what was in the works. Whatever it was, it was worth it to see Charlie's gleeful curiosity. He'd been moping all week, acting out in school, and it wasn't hard to guess why.

"What?" Charlie skidded around the back of the car to peer inside. Mason waited for a squeal, or a laugh, or anything, but only silence met his ears. Dana looked over the trunk hood at him, a worried look on her face.

Charlie crawled up onto the bumper as Mason came around the back fender of the car and felt himself grow as speechless as his son. There, set up inside a flat cardboard box in the trunk of the little car, was a pond.

It was little—more of a garden ornament than anything else, not even big enough to be called a fishpond. A fountain, really. A wide cement dish with uneven edges like a pond, small metal lily pads decorating part of the edge. A comical ceramic frog perched on one corner, the little metal tube coming out of his mouth show-ing where water would spout into the pond.

A pond. Dana had bought Charlie a pond. His own pond, exactly when he needed it. Mason nearly leaned against the car, overcome with awe and gratitude. No words could make it past the knot in his throat. When Charlie gently touched the little frog Mason thought he'd never find words to convey the multiple emotions threatening his composure.

"It's too much, I know," Dana gushed, one hand ner-vously tucking her hair behind one ear. "But I didn't pay for it. Hannah and I saw it in the window and I went in to buy it but Mike wouldn't let me. I figured… I hoped…"

"You got me a pond!" Charlie cut in, eyes wide. In those five words, and the look on his son's face, Mason knew it was going to be okay. At least for now. "I got a pond!" he repeated to Mason.

"It's tiny, but…"

Mason simply grabbed Dana's hand, lost for any suf-ficient words. "It's perfect," he managed after a mound of effort. "Thank you."

"Flowers are being delivered tomorrow. Hannah talked Lorna at the flower shop into it. Pond-sized ones, I think. Well, *this* pond-sized ones. This isn't really a pond, is it?"

Mason considered the small army of people Dana had recruited to make this happen and thought he might lose it. What was it they said about God being able to do more than we can hope or imagine? Proof of it was standing in front of him. A solution he couldn't find a way to see, but Dana had seen it and brought it to him.

Mason gave her hand another squeeze and then let it go, fearing he might hug her if he held on any longer.

"So it's…okay?" Her voice wavered as she wiped her eyes with the back of her hand.

He could only nod. It was so much more than okay. It was an answer to a desperate prayer.

"We can put it under the tree off the porch," Charlie said, peering into the trunk to view the pond from different angles. "There's a pump so we'll need electricity. We can do that, can't we, Dad?"

"Sure," Mason choked out.

"And we get flowers tomorrow? Did you say that?" Charlie asked Dana.

Dana nodded, swallowing hard. "I don't know which kind, though."

"Doesn't matter," Charlie said with an amazing simplicity. To him, the problem had been solved. It had, hadn't it? Mason couldn't help but feel that maybe, just maybe, they were turning a corner on this thing.

Because of Dana. The wonder of that scared him to death.

Chapter Ten

It was sweet and sad and amazing, all at the same time.

Dana stood with Charlie and Mason in front of the little ornamental pond the next afternoon, the amusing ceramic frog spouting his continual stream into the water. It was a peaceful, soothing sound, standing out against the dusty landscape all around them. With a pang she remembered the sight of the pond—or what used to be the pond—that she made a point to find as she drove off the property yesterday. That wide circle of dried and caked mud that felt so lonely and barren. The thought of Charlie's memories of his mother's treasured tradition drying up with that pond had brought tears to her eyes.

The thought of being able to put this tiny piece of Charlie and Mason's life to rights threatened a new surge of tears as they stood solemnly for a moment.

"Do you remember what to do?" Mason asked. Dana could hear the man's own emotions thicken his words. If the sight of the lost pond had struck her so hard, how could it have been any less difficult for him? It wasn't lack of caring, or searching for a solution, that kept Mason from coming up with what to do. It was the sheer overwhelm of grief. She was no stranger to that, or the helplessness it too often fed.

"I remember," Charlie said. He bent down to the small box of beautiful, tropical-looking flowers Mason told her had arrived that morning. Four lovely blooms, each trimmed from their stems so that they would float in the water. "Which is for which?" he asked Mason.

"You get to decide," Mason answered. "Do you need help with the names?"

Charlie shook his head. "Nope, I got 'em."

The three of them stood silent for a moment as Charlie seemed to ponder his next step. Dana couldn't remember the last time she could describe a moment as sacred. Still, the simple little tradition touched her far more deeply than she was ready to accept. It honored her—and frightened her—to be here, and yet she felt certain she was supposed to be here. That it had been no accident she'd been at Mason's house to hear about the incident and help sort through Charlie's feelings. That she'd been meant to walk by that store window and see the little ornamental pond. Camp True North Springs was a big thing she was being swept up in, but this was a small, personal thing where she felt the same sense of being pulled in. It felt deeply right—and she hadn't felt deeply right about anything in far too long.

Charlie picked up a purple flower with starlike petals. "We remember Tutu Kane." He paused and looked up at Dana. "That's my grandpa."

With a heartbreaking solemnity, Charlie placed the flower in the water. It made a small circle of ripples that danced to meet the ripples of the fountain stream. Dana swallowed hard and she heard Mason clear his throat. She didn't feel safe to meet the man's eyes—it must be such a painful, private moment for him.

"We remember Tutu Wa… Wahi…"

"Wahine," Mason offered softly.

"Tutu Wahine," Charlie said, placing a coral-colored flower of the same shape into the water. "That's Grandma." The bloom floated toward the first one until the petals touched briefly, bobbing together in the small pond. "Look," Charlie pronounced, "they're holding hands."

"They always did." Mason sounded as if he could barely get the words out. "Why not now?"

"I think they like this pond. It's not the same as the old one, but that's okay."

There wasn't a single statement that would have made Dana feel more grateful that she'd given in to this irrational impulse. She blinked away tears as Charlie selected a different bloom from the two left in the box.

"We remember Grandpa," the boy said as he placed the flower in the water with care. Dana saw Mason put a hand to his chest. Charlie had talked about his grandmother coming in from Flagstaff for Special Ladies Day. Evidently Mason's father had passed away sometime earlier. She had always felt as though one of the worst parts of her police work was the sheer volume of violence and death she'd been witness to. But volume, while daunting, held nothing against the personal nature of these losses. Charlie and Mason had seen so much loss. No wonder losing the pond this year struck such a deep blow.

There was only one flower left in the box. A beautiful blossom, bright pink and larger than the others. There was no doubt who this bloom was for. Dana felt a tear slip down her cheek as Charlie paused a moment, pulling in a telling breath before he picked up the flower and set it with tender care into the water. "We remember Mama." His brave little voice cracked a bit on the declaration, and Dana heard the small sound of Mason holding in his own sorrow. Sacred moments indeed. Hard as it was, she was glad to be here. Honored to be here, and to have played a part of making this moment happen.

Every kid's visit here should end with something like this, she thought.

Bring the pond back. It took Dana a few seconds to realize that wasn't just a thought, it was a prayer. She wasn't even sure she had gained any of her faith back, and here she was asking the Almighty to move the forces of nature for one pond on one plot of land in Arizona. Was that an okay thing to ask of the God she'd left behind for so many years?

The span of silence as they all gazed at the quartet of floating flowers was broken only by the occasional sniffle or sigh. Words weren't needed—what words could contain all that sorrow anyway? Dana fought the urge to put a hand on Mason's shoulder, to somehow offer a wordless show of support. But even though she was here, it was a private moment. Touching Mason felt like intruding. She was really here to stand witness, and that was honor enough. Or it ought to be. Dana told herself the strong pull she felt to be closer to him was merely compassion, grief recognizing grief.

But every cop gets good at spotting lies. It was more than that. It was care. A deep, surprising, scary care that raised the stakes of everything about Camp True North Springs. About her and why she was here.

Without any further ceremony, Charlie sat down to watch the four blooms float slowly around in the tiny current made by the fountain. There was such a lovely peace about it that she sat down beside Charlie. Her memory cast back to the words of one of the songs in Marion's well-worn hymnal that talked about peace like a river. Peace like a pond? Why not? Nothing about any of this adventure made a normal kind of sense.

Dana waited for Mason to sit down on Charlie's other side, but he did not. He remained standing. She could feel him shifting his feet behind her, hear his labored breathing. The weight of this moment for him must be tremendous. She realized she wanted the pond to come back, the peace and the healing, for him as much as for Charlie. Perhaps realize wasn't the right word. She'd known it for some time now, so maybe admitted was a better word. She wouldn't act on it—not yet and maybe not ever—but here, beside the pond and the memories, it felt safe to admit it.

Charlie put his finger in the water and swished it around, sending the flowers dancing across the surface of the little pond. It seemed to infuse a tiny bit of joy in all the sadness. After a moment, Charlie held the wet finger up to Dana and asked, "Wanna?"

Her heart swelled with the boy's invitation into his

tradition. Dana placed a finger in the water and wiggled it, astonished to feel a smile come to her face. They spent a few moments sending the flowers on little trips across and around the water. Then Charlie gave a small sigh, said a simple "Thanks," and, to Dana's total surprise, leaned his head against her shoulder.

The gentle movement struck her like thunder. "You're so very welcome," she managed to choke out behind the tears piling up in her throat. One stole down her cheek again and she tried to wipe it away without disturbing Charlie.

She was doing fine holding it together until she felt a pressure on her other shoulder. Mason's hand. The warmth of it, the tentative nature of the touch, the mountain of emotion behind it—it flooded through Dana with even more force than Charlie's gesture. Mason gave the slightest of squeezes, and she heard the wordless thank you loud and clear.

Dana took her hand, still wet from both the pond and her tears, and placed it on top of Mason's. She didn't care whether it was appropriate or invasive.

Because she cared. And right now, that was more important than anything.

Mason stared at Dana's hand on top of his and felt his world tilt sideways. She'd done this astounding thing, somehow managing to find the one way out of today's mess. A way he couldn't hope to find.

He was beyond grateful for what she'd done.

But he was also grateful *for* her. For who she was. Dana had somehow kept her warrior spirit even while wounded, whereas he had…what? Given up, if he was honest. Let himself grow cold and hard at what life had dealt him. He didn't want that for Charlie, and that meant Dana was right—he needed to restore his own spirit in order to nurture his son's.

After today, he could no longer shake the notion that Dana was the key to that. *But I'm not ready*, his heart cried out. *I'm still too broken.*

You're ready to heal, his weary soul answered his thoughts. He looked at the floating flowers, bobbing and touching in no real pattern but beautiful anyway. *It's already started, right here. Can't you feel it?*

Charlie broke the solemnity of the moment. "Can we have the brownies now?" He swiveled his head around to view Mason, catching the position of his and Dana's hands. Charlie's eyes widened, and Dana and Mason both pulled their hands away as if burned. Mason felt the skin on his neck and jaw heat up.

"Sure, buddy," Mason said, trying to sound normal. Maybe Charlie didn't pick up on the magnitude of the moment, but he knew Dana had. She caught his gaze as she went to get up off the ground, and he knew that touch had crossed a line. Could he go back? Did he want to?

"Rita sent over some brownies with Lorna's delivery of flowers," he explained, just to fill the awkward air between them. "Seems like half the town's in on this thing." Knowing so many people went to such lengths to try and help his family made Mason feel both loved and indebted. The combination of feelings prickled under his skin—and around his heart.

"That's so nice," Dana said, sounding just as awkward. Just what was this thing growing between them? How should they handle the way it was getting stronger? Mason was pretty sure neither of them had an answer. "Rita makes good brownies."

Charlie had already risen and was dusting off his hands on his pants. "I make good popcorn. Dad makes good spaghetti. What do you make?" He addressed his question to Dana, somehow convinced everyone had a culinary specialty.

She didn't. And somehow, in the face of this extraordinary tradition Charlie's mother had instilled and the homey sense of the woman that permeated the house, that felt like a major fault. Dana scrambled for an answer, coming up with "I make good coffee?"

Charlie rolled his eyes. "Well, that's no good."

"Charlie!" Mason called out his son's brutal honesty.

"He's right," Dana said, shrugging. "Totally useless in the second grade." And then she started to laugh. It was a small, tense laugh at first, nervous and thin. But it didn't stay that way. She made an "ick" face at Charlie, who made an even bigger "ick" face right back, and soon the three of them were laughing way harder than the small joke deserved.

The laughter was like the ripples in the little pond— they reverberated back on themselves, doubling and joining as they expanded. Mason laughed until his eyes teared, until Charlie rolled on the ground and Dana sat back on her elbows.

Maybe Mason didn't have the beauty of the floating flowers. Maybe he was just the goofy ceramic frog putting his own brand of ripples into the pond. Suddenly the little garden pond was as much about him as it was about Charlie.

As it was about Dana.

They sat in the kitchen sharing brownies—and coffee Charlie insisted Dana make to prove her boast. Charlie of course had milk but insisted on tasting a small sip of Dana's coffee before declaring it "double ick" even though Mason found it pretty good. Still, the afternoon had been pulled back from its earlier sad seriousness. It felt close to ordinary, and that was a gift.

When it came time for Dana to go, Mason found himself at a loss for what to say about all she'd done. Thank you didn't come close, but he feared going too far into all the things he was feeling. "You saved us today. You saved me."

She seemed to consider his words for a moment. "Actually, today saved me, too. I haven't felt like I've made a difference—to anyone—since the shooting. It felt really good to make this happen for Charlie. Not just me, of course, all those people."

Mostly you, Mason wanted to add, but stayed silent. Such a storm of feelings was raging in his chest it felt like he wouldn't sleep for days. It was chaotic, but it also felt alive. It had been so long since he could say he felt like he was doing anything close to living.

"What's the next step with the camp?" He wasn't ready to say yes—inching closer, but not all the way there. Still, after today, Mason felt he owed her the chance to move her exploration forward.

She seemed so pleased by the question. "Architect

concept drawings. You know, something concrete to show a committee. That sort of thing."

He felt a smile creep across his face. "Your stuff isn't already detailed enough?" She had it all planned out down to most of the details from where he stood.

"Not for our friends at planning and zoning. They need lots of the utilities stuff ironed out. Electric, water, drainage, safety and such."

Again, he liked the easy way she said *our*. It was nice to have something—even a hypothetical something—where it wasn't all on his shoulders.

"I've got an architect picked out. Are you ready for something like that?"

Was he ready? Who knew. But he felt like trying it on for size, and that had to be worth something. "I suppose."

She grinned at what he knew she'd call a victory. He didn't mind giving her that victory, either. Mason thought it would feel like giving in, but it didn't. It felt like opening up, if that made any sense.

"I'll set up the appointment for next week and let you know."

"Good."

Dana shrugged again, as if they didn't know what to say or how to end the conversation. "Okay then. See you soon."

"Sure. And thanks again. Really. It's…amazing, the pond."

They said an awkward goodbye, skittishly avoiding touching each other even though his hand still hummed with the memory of hers atop his. It stunned him how much he felt her absence as her car rumbled down the drive. As he walked past the little pond on his way back to the front porch, he stopped and touched one finger to the still-spouting frog and his bulging tin eyes. *Maybe I am ready.*

Charlie was on the front room couch when he got back into the house, on his knees as if he'd been watching the whole thing through the window. Mason didn't know what to make of that.

"I like her," Charlie pronounced, twisting to bounce on the cushion. "I didn't at first, but I do now. And not just 'cuz of my pond—although that's pretty neat."

Mason sat down next to his son. "It is. Feeling better about everything?"

"Some." Charlie paused for an unnatural moment, a second-grader's attempt at seeming casual. "Do *you* like her?"

How to answer that? He settled for "She's nice."

"She's funny." He sunk back into the cushions. "Can you explain the camp thing again to me?"

Mason gave his best simplistic explanation of what it was Dana was trying to do, this time clarifying that Camp True North Springs would be at their house, on their property. He made sure to let Charlie know that no one had decided to go ahead with anything. Yet. Charlie listened and asked a few questions.

"Here? At our house?"

"That's the thing," Mason said. "It'd be right here, not near here. It's a good idea, but it would change our house. Forever."

"I like our house," Charlie said, looking around.

Mason sat back as well, feeling the weight of the emotional day press him into the cushions. "I do, too."

"So I'd live at a camp? Kids would come live with us?"

"More like visit," Mason corrected. "We'd keep this house for us to live in, but it'd be like having lots of company over. Kids and moms and dads who've been through what we've been through." Mason suddenly realized he couldn't quite say if he was promoting the idea to Charlie or himself. And when had he started promoting the idea at all?

"Would Dana live here?"

"No," Mason replied quickly. "We'd be like…business partners. She'd be here a lot, I suppose every day, but I don't think she'd live here." They'd never discussed it, and quite honestly the thought of her so close on a continual basis did things to his pulse that had nothing to do with the quality of her coffee.

"Oh," said Charlie, surprisingly disappointed.

"You *want* her to live here?" Mason couldn't believe he was asking his son that question.

"I dunno. Prob'ly not if she's no good at cooking. All those kids gotta eat, right?"

Mason could only imagine Dana's cringe had she heard that. "I think we'd hire a cook." The word "we" had come out of his mouth before he'd had time to stop it.

"A cook? Like one who could make birthday cakes? And lasagna? And tacos?" Charlie clearly thought this was great.

"Hold on there, buddy. We're getting ahead of ourselves. Like I said, no one has said yes to anything yet."

Charlie pivoted so that his head was in Mason's lap. He swung his feet up to hang over the arm of the couch, draped over the furniture like some kind of tiny teenager. "You should," he said. As if it were that simple. "What're you scared of?"

Mason groped for an equally simple answer. "Lots of things would change around here if I did."

"I know. I get it."

His son's acceptance stunned him. "You think I should?" This wasn't the kind of decision that should be made on the advice of a seven-year-old. Or was it?

"Yep."

Mason felt his world shift a little further out of the gloomy past.

Chapter Eleven

The following Tuesday, Dana watched Mason walk up the sidewalk to the front steps of Theo Anderson's architectural office just off the town square. She tried to fight her grin at the fact that Mason was wearing a shirt and tie. Up until now, she'd never seen him in anything but work or casual clothes. Since this was a business meeting, however, his choice of dress made an endearing sort of sense. She ignored the small surge of attraction she felt toward him in the spiffy attire— Mason Avery cleaned up very nice. She'd found him handsome in his more rugged attire, but she wondered if he knew what a stunner he was dressed up. Naturally, it wasn't for her, but for the business nature of the meeting. She'd gone for a crisp pantsuit herself, wanting to make a good impression—on Theo, of course.

Despite the storm of nerves in her own stomach, Dana thought she caught a hint of admiration as Mason took in her wardrobe choice. They were learning new things about each other, that was for certain.

She clutched her file like a shield against the loud drum of her pulse. "You're sure?" She had to ask again. Agreeing to this meeting with an architect to draw up preliminary plans felt like such a huge leap forward.

"If I'm honest, no," he said, offering a shrug. "But I'm ready to think harder about it. And I know Theo." Mason pulled the entrance door open for her, waving her inside. Dana couldn't remember the last time anyone at the precinct opened a door for her. Equality on the force was a good thing, but there was something to be said for good old-fashioned manners in North Springs.

Mason's familiarity with Theo had to be a good sign, right? Theo was on her side, and Theo could help convince Mason. If this meeting went the way she hoped it would, it was entirely possible that all the necessary paperwork could be submitted by next week. Next week! The possibility of that lit a fire in her.

As they headed down the hall to Anderson's office, Dana asked "How's Charlie?" before they reached the door.

"I haven't had a call from the vice principal or Mrs. Booker," Mason replied. "I call that a win. And we sit out by Franco every night after dinner."

She raised an eyebrow in his direction. "Franco?"

Mason nodded. "Evidently the frog has a name now."

The idea made Dana absurdly happy. She ran her thumb along the tab of the file that said "Camp True North Springs." Names were important. Names made things real, and yours.

Theo Anderson was a tall, tan man with neat blond hair and serious-looking glasses. "Mason," he said, extending a hand. "Good to see you." He turned his gaze to Dana. "Miss Preston. The lady with the plan. You certainly meet my appetite for details."

She shook his hand, suddenly worried about the multiple files she'd emailed over. "Too much?"

Theo led them to a small conference room. "No such thing in my business. I wish all my clients had your dedication to details."

"Years of police paperwork will do that to a person." Dana felt so clumsy at making this kind of small talk. If this camp was going to require a lot of glad-handing— schmoozing as one of the guys on the force often called it—she feared she was going to come up short.

"Law enforcement," Theo said, nodding. "That explains a lot. I expect you've seen a lot in your day that makes the case for a place like this." He pulled a file in front of him, and Dana felt a small zing at the sight of "Camp True North Springs" neatly typed on the label.

He opened the file and pulled out the plat of survey Mason told her he'd been asked to send over. Or, more precisely a copy of it, since it now had red markings all over it. The drawing seemed to show what transformations would be required of each of the buildings, as well as the position of the three new buildings that would need to be erected. The camp was now a concrete plan on someone's desk, not just a handful of sketches in her head and notebooks. Something close to momentum began to build in Dana's chest.

Theo turned to Mason. "I don't mind saying I think this is a great idea. Good use of that huge parcel. I've been worried about you and Charlie banging around that big place all by yourselves. Dad says he thinks your grandparents would have been in favor of something like this."

Mason seemed startled by that. "You talked to your folks about this?"

"I didn't realize that would be a problem. I wanted to get a gauge of community reaction, especially from people who know your family."

Dana felt her sense of momentum sputter to a crawl. Was Mason not as open to this as she'd thought? He didn't want anyone to know he was considering this—that had to be a bad sign.

"I'm just not fully…committed at this point," Mason was too quick to counter. "I'm still deciding. But I'm okay with exploring it."

Dana would have liked a little more enthusiasm from Mason. Still, this whole thing represented a huge change in his life. He was right to be taking it slow despite her urgency.

"Okay then," answered Theo. "We'll keep things under wraps for now. But once this goes before the zoning board, it'll be public. You want me to keep going?"

Dana waited for Mason's tentative nod before she replied, "Keep going."

"The good news is almost everything works in your favor," Theo began. "No flood plain issues, the right amount of land, only a few new structures. Plumbing and electric are the most complicated, but they always are. The big hurdle is getting the land rezoned to commercial use from residential use."

"Figured that," Mason said.

"Since you're not building a giant condo development, that's an easier climb." He turned to Dana. "Have you spoken with the state office about registering as a nonprofit yet?"

"Not yet," Dana replied. "It's on my list."

"Start that now. Takes a while, and it might help at the zoning hearings."

"Hearings?" Dana didn't like the sound of that.

"Smaller things—chimneys, fences, parking lots—go through without a hearing unless there's someone against it. Rezoning like this can be a bit more complicated. There's always someone sure you're putting a ding in their property values."

"Nicholson," Mason said.

Everyone seemed to bring up Arthur Nicholson as the largest obstacle in her plan. Still, given the nature of some of the goons she'd come up against in Denver, Dana wasn't about to let some guy derail everything she'd accomplished so far.

"Arthur will be an obstacle, yes. I can't see him voting in favor of this. And he has a loud mouth when he doesn't like something."

"But he's only one vote," Dana protested. "There are seven people on the zoning committee, right?"

Theo nodded, impressed. "She does her homework."

"She does everybody's homework," Mason said. It was the closest thing to a joke he'd made the entire meeting. "Except Charlie's."

Theo sat back. "Actually, if you don't mind my saying so, I think Charlie could be key here."

Mason stiffened. "We keep Charlie out of this."

Dana was torn on how to react. This was, in all kinds of ways, about Charlie. And kids like Charlie whose lives had been torn by violence they never chose. Or chose because they didn't know there were other choices. And yet she understood Mason's desire to protect his son.

"What happened to Melony makes this very personal for North Springs," Theo explained. "I think that's important. Folks like Arthur will try to make this out as some kind of gang member summer camp, nothing they want near their homes. Someone's going to bring up that squabble over the rehab center a year back."

Dana looked at Mason and Theo. "Squabble?" That didn't sound helpful.

"A rehab center opened on the west side of town about a year ago," Theo explained. "One guy got out of hand and some people—Nicholson included—made way too much of it. Claiming they were importing troublemakers, that sort of thing. You and Charlie are two of our own. I think Charlie's welfare shows the other side of the issue."

"Nobody's going to make Charlie some Camp True North Springs poster boy."

The edge in Mason's words sliced at Dana's heart like a blade. She didn't want that. Not for any child, and especially not for Charlie. Charlie would not, *could* not pay a price for her dream.

"Of course not," she tried to assure him. "I don't want that any more than you do. Sure, Charlie is the one child they know, but we need to find a way to tell people that Charlie is so far from the only one. We're welcoming victims, not importing troublemakers. So many families are reeling from what violence has done to someone they love. I could tell you so many stories..."

"Then you should," Theo said.

"What?" Dana asked.

"You should tell those stories." Theo leaned in. "I know I may be getting ahead of things here, but I really think it's possible to get the whole community—or most of it—behind this idea. This is a pretty big undertaking, but it's a compelling one. The more folks from town you get in your corner, the easier all of this is going to be."

"The pond, just bigger," Dana said, warming to the idea.

"Huh?" Theo asked.

Dana started to launch in about the amazing tale of all the people who pitched in to give Charlie his pond tradition this year. Instead, something told her to hold back and let Mason tell it. She nodded at him, and while reluctant at first, he did relay the story of Franco the frog, his quirky little pond, the flowers, how Mike and Rita and Hannah and a bunch of other people leapt at the chance to pitch in. All of the emotion of the day came back to both her and Mason, she could feel it.

Even Theo was visibly moved by the story. "That," he said. "That's what I mean. True North Springs at its very core. It's what really makes our town the place we love. Not Arthur's ordinances or zoning laws or parking or traffic or any of that stuff."

Mason's face reflected the same trepidation that landed hard in Dana's stomach. Feeling the urge to help these kids, these families, was one thing. One thing they'd shared between the two of them. And it had worked out with the small circle of those who'd made the pond happen. But to spread it out to all of North Springs? That was another thing altogether. Big. And really, really unnerving, no matter how called she felt to the idea.

And yet Theo was right. It was going to happen at some point, and the more they could pull people into the vision for Camp True North Springs, the stronger the chances of it coming to life. It was always about more than just Charlie—although Charlie had become such a big piece of it for her. Now it needed to become about more than just her and Mason.

"I've got an idea," Theo said, raising a hopeful eyebrow and casting his glance back and forth between her and Mason. "I think we should take a page from the Busketeers' playbook. Are you ready to hear it?"

Mason stood in the gazebo a few days later and tried to calm his clanging nerves. Theo's idea to pull the Busketeers into hosting a Saturday morning pancake breakfast to introduce the idea of Camp True North Springs had caught like wildfire. He tried to take that instant wave of support as a sign, but too much of him doubted it. Some terrified part of him felt as if this wild idea of Dana's was quickly hijacking his family heritage, stealing the acres out from underneath his and Charlie's feet.

And yet another part of him remained so grateful to feel anything at all. Even feeling caught up in *something* was better than the numb stagnation that had plagued him since Melony's death. He'd felt a great deal—too much—that day beside the little pond. Today loomed as if it would flood him the same way. *It's just an idea,* he kept trying to tell himself. *You still haven't said yes to anything yet. It's just an idea.*

No, it wasn't just an idea. It was something that had lodged deep within him, tugging at him. Pretty soon he wouldn't be able to fight it off.

Speaking of tugging, Charlie was yanking on his sleeve. "Look at all the people, Dad." In truth, there were more here today than at the barbecue the other night. "What's 'ordinaried' mean, anyway?"

Mason looked down at him. "'Ordinaried'? I don't think that's a real word."

Charlie scrunched up his face. "Mr. Bart used it. About today. But I think he said it different." He tried again. "'Orphayned'?"

"That's not a word, either." With a bit of a shiver, Mason realized the word Charlie was mispronouncing. "Ordained?"

"Yeah, that's it. Ordained. What's it mean?"

There really was only one definition, and it didn't help Mason's uneasiness. "It means something God planned. Something He thinks ought to happen so He blesses it to help make it happen." Even his own definition seemed to convict him of the thing he was trying so hard not to admit.

"But it's Miss Dana who started all this. Is she ordained? Is that a special thing?"

Mason had to wonder what Dana would make of such a statement. "Miss Dana is special, but she is an ordinary person like you and me." Even as he said it, the small-but-growing voice in his own heart argued that Dana Preston was anything but ordinary. "But God can use any kind of person to accomplish His purpose. I think Mr. Bart was saying that God might be paving the way for the camp to happen."

God paving the way for Camp True North Springs. God bringing Dana Preston here to North Springs, to his land and his world of grief, for this to happen. It seemed too grand a thought. The kind of thing that would happen to someone with a far more spiritual strength than he seemed to have right now. A Moses-part-the-Red-Sea-sized idea—and he was a far cry from any Moses.

As if to underscore that doubt, Mason caught sight of Arthur Nicholson walking toward him at a speed that could only be described as combat-ready. "Go find Miss Dana," he told Charlie, "see if she needs any help with anything." The scowl on Nicholson's face told him this might not be a conversation Charlie ought to hear.

He was rather surprised Nicholson had shown up, actually. Then again, the man liked to make sure he was seen at most community events. He didn't have a plate in his hands, so he wasn't here for the Busketeers' cooking. Mason didn't care for the sharp but carefully civil edge in his stare. "Getting a bit ahead of ourselves, don't you think, Avery?"

The fact that Mason had entertained the same thought—repeatedly—didn't make it pleasant to hear Nicholson say it. "It's just a breakfast, Arthur. Nothing's set."

"Looks awfully set to me. Trying to lobby the zoning committee ahead of even submitting the request, perhaps? Didn't put you down for that kind of politicking."

That kind of politicking was what Arthur Nicholson loved, in Mason's opinion. "Nope. Not that at all. Just letting people try the idea on for size."

"Can't say I care for the idea. We should have learned our lesson from the rehab center. It'd be a mistake to bring in underprivileged kids from crime-ridden cities here to our town for some prize of a holiday."

Wow. Had Arthur spent hours thinking of the meanest, most misguided way to describe what was going on here? A surge of defensive anger stiffened Mason's spine.

"Doing something for families *of all kinds* who have had violence tear a great big hole in their lives? Giving victims a chance to catch their breath and heal?" Mason shot back, not bothering to soften the edge in his own voice. "Families like *mine*?" His instant personalization of the issue surprised him. It wasn't that Arthur referred to it as "his" idea that raised his hackles, it was the vicious way Arthur described it.

Mason realized he had taken ownership of the idea, right alongside Dana. Arthur simply helped him recognize it. He was wrong back in Theo's office. This *had* to be about him and Charlie. It *had always* been about him and Charlie. "Is that what you're saying, Arthur?" Mason pressed, glaring at the man.

Arthur gave an ugly snort. "Please. You and I both know who's going to show up if you do this thing."

Mason turned to square off at Arthur. "No, Arthur. I don't. Why don't you tell me?" A bitter part of him wanted to force Nicholson to voice his prejudices, to own up to the way he looked down his nose at people.

In fact, Mason and Dana had gone over a careful selection of stories she was going to tell. Stories that showed desperate city kids and well-off suburban kids. Big families and tiny ones like he and Charlie. Stories that showed the loss he was living with didn't care about your bank account or your neighborhood. Violence was an equal opportunity predator, stealing from all sorts.

"Problem kids. Drugs. Gangs. Nothing North Springs wants on its doorstep. Leave that stuff to the big cities. We don't need it here."

Mason huffed. "Oh, of course. We have no problems here in our perfect little town. We can't contaminate ourselves with problem children." Something fierce came over Mason—Dana's warrior spirit, it felt like—and he stepped closer to Arthur. "I guess I should go tell Charlie he's somehow managed to lose his mother in the wrong zip code. Violence is a big-city problem."

"You don't have to get that way," Arthur replied, chin jutting out.

"No, evidently I do," Mason replied. "I hope you stay for the discussion, Arthur. You need to hear it."

"Oh, I've heard all I need to hear." With that, Arthur turned on his polished heels and headed back toward his office on the far side of the square.

Something settled hard and solid at the base of Mason's spine. Without even making the decision to do so, he'd just become one hundred percent committed to Camp True North Springs. Not for Dana—although she was a large part of it, to be sure. Not even for Charlie—although he was a powerful reason. It was for him. Himself.

The numb, near-hopeless shell he'd built up, the one

Dana had been chipping away at since she showed up insistent and invasive at his front gate, had just cracked wide open. Mason could almost hear it crashing into bits at his feet, the sensation was that powerful. *Released.* That was the only word for how he felt. Now, coming roaring out with a force that quite frankly scared him, was a man he'd thought long gone. A man with energy and purpose and something to fight for instead of just surviving. No way, no how was Mason going to let someone like Arthur Nicholson stand in the way of his return to life.

Breathing hard, reeling and exhilarated and wound up all at the same time, Mason scanned the square for Dana. The need to find her, to ground himself in her steady gaze before whatever this was took him over, surged up. *Find Dana.* He wanted her hand on his shoulder the way he'd placed his hand on hers back at Franco's little pond. He couldn't, of course—that would be a spectacularly bad idea right now, in front of all these people. But after this morning was over, he'd find a way to tell her. To let her know he would now fight as fiercely and relentlessly for Camp True North Springs as she would.

Arthur and his kind would not win. *So help me God. So please, help me, God.*

Chapter Twelve

"Emilio got his high school GED and went to trade school. He's doing okay. But he never fully recovered from what happened that night. And he lost so many good years and so many chances." Dana scanned the crowd as she told this last of four stories, trying to meet the eyes of everyone listening to her. "He'd tell you he listened to the wrong guy, mostly because there were no other voices talking to him in the midst of his grief and anger. That the only choice anyone ever offered him was to fight back. You know," Dana felt her throat tighten the way it always did when she told Emilio's story, "he once said to me, 'I was a loaded weapon long before anyone put a gun in my hands.' I've never forgotten that."

She sat back down on the small stool they had placed in front of the gazebo steps. "We seem to have forgotten that weapons can be unloaded. Bombs can be defused. I've seen a lot of ugliness in my day. Things I expect most of you would call evil. And yeah, there were those people who fit that word. But mostly what I see are kids with wounds. Who can't see choices. Or possibilities beyond 'hurt him before he hurts you more.'"

Dana tried to read the expressions of the people listening. Usually, she was good at that sort of thing, well-trained to read an environment. The trouble was, she kept being distracted by the huge change she saw in Mason. He was completely, utterly changed from the cautious man in Theo's office. He was even different from the man who'd walked onto the square this morning with an "I'm not sure we'll pull this off" expression.

Now he stood off to one side, absolutely radiating conviction. Purpose gave his eyes a new clarity. His feet seemed to plant themselves firmly on the ground. His shoulders pulled back to make him stand even taller. His hands nearly fisted when they used to hide in his pockets. Someone had lit Mason Avery on fire, and it was a thrilling thing to see.

A large part of her wanted to believe it had been *her* that transformed him, and for reasons that went far beyond Camp True North Springs. She'd seen tiny glimpses of this new Mason, become convinced the man she saw now was indeed buried deep within the lifeless man she'd been seeing before. *I wanted to be the one to rescue him*, she dared to admit to herself. *I wanted to bring him back to life.*

She'd come to care for him and Charlie in ways that seemed dangerous right now. So much more personal—and confusing—than just transforming the property. Something told her that if she did take even a step in that direction with Mason, there'd be no going back. That there was no halfway on this, no safety net or shield. If things went wrong on a personal level between her and Mason—and there seemed to be a million ways that could happen—it would all come crashing down. All of it.

She couldn't do that to herself, or the camp, or Mason, or most especially to Charlie.

A woman's raised hand brought her back to the moment. "Why here?" the woman asked.

Dana could cite a dozen logistical reasons, but she knew it had to go deeper than that. "It could be anywhere, really. Anyplace with sky and space and people willing to show up and care. But it does need a certain size property with people already on it, willing to make the renovations." She shrugged, unable to find another way to convey her final reason. "And I was drawn here. In a way I trust but can't quite explain."

That seemed a silly way to explain it. Too touchy-feely for practical, salt-of-the-earth people like those in North Springs. After all, Dana wasn't even sure she understood it herself.

Rita stood up and faced the crowd. "Well, no one needs to explain it to me. God drew you here. Mason is so ready to make this happen the man is practically vibrating in his boots. It's the best idea I've heard in ages. I'm in."

A few people nodded in agreement, but just as many looked around warily. Cautious murmurs rippled through the gathering.

"It's needed," Bart added, standing as well. "We've seen it in small ways here, and bigger ways on the news." The Busketeer shifted his gaze to Charlie. "Maybe even in big ways here. I think we ought to do this."

"But it's not us," said a man Dana recognized from the bank. "It's Mason. We don't really have to get involved. How many kids are you gonna have up there on the mountain anyway? Hundreds?"

"A dozen at a time, maybe twenty," Dana said. "Small groups. This isn't going to be some kind of big institution."

"But they'll be here," the man pressed. "In town at some point. We all saw that with the rehab center and no one wants more of that."

"It's not as if they're moving in," Hannah said. "They're visitors. We have visitors all the time. We claim we welcome visitors. We have pretty brochures that claim we love visitors. Here's a chance to act like we really mean that."

"You could bring them to church," Rita said, speaking directly to Mason this time. If there was ever any question that this was Dana's idea alone, that was long gone as of today. They were now a partnership. She tried not to think about the warm glow that set off under her skin. "In fact, I hope you do bring them to church. We could show them such a warm welcome. Think what that could do."

"Until they start breaking our car windows," another man said. "They'd be here because nobody taught them right from wrong. Why does it have to be our job?"

Dana was trying to figure out how to answer such a judgmental statement when Rita whirled on the man. "Davis Taylor," she said, calling him out like a schoolmarm. "Tell me I did not just hear such an uncharitable thing come out of your churchgoing mouth." She wagged her finger so hard at Davis that the crowd broke into nervous laughter. Still, Dana could tell, he'd only voiced what several of them were thinking.

"I understand your concerns," Dana said. "Violence does often lead to violence. But there are ways to stop the cycle. To catch a child or a family before they *react* and teach them how to *respond*. Show them other choices. New possibilities. It's worked in other places."

"So let them go there," someone called from the back of the crowd. The mean taunt doused all the remaining glow in Dana's chest, stinging as much as her scar had in the early days after her surgery. "We don't want that here."

He'd had enough. Mason raised his voice to boom across the crowd. "Maybe *I* think it should be here. On *my* land. All I really need from you all is the zoning variance." Honestly, at this moment, Mason felt as if he'd do it whether the zoning committee gave him permission or not. "If you all decide you never want these kids to darken the door of your perfect little town, I'll live with it."

He'd never called North Springs "your little town" before. This town had been home to his family for three generations. That mountain land had been Avery land since Grandpa's day. *His* North Springs would get behind the camp. And if they didn't, he wasn't quite sure how he could think of the town as his any longer.

The anger and energy seemed to roar up in him from out of nowhere, from some pent-up reservoir of determination. What had solidified his stance this fast?

He didn't know, and he didn't much care. He was making up for lost time, and no one—Arthur Nicholson or otherwise—was going to stand in his way now.

Mason walked down to the front of the group. He stood at the bottom of the stairs underneath where Dana had been seated telling her stories. "But think about this. Some of the kids who will come here are what you'd call problems. But don't all kids have problems? Every adult I know has problems. That's nothing new to the world, nothing new to North Springs, and you know it. Don't you tell me some kids in this community haven't had a rough go of it through no fault of their own."

Mason looked straight at Willy's mother. Willy's dad was gone more than he was home, and she worked two jobs to make ends meet. He looked at Brenda Summers, holding her gaze even when she tried to look away. He had no doubt Brenda had used the word "problem" in describing Charlie. "But some of these kids are families like Charlie and me. *Just* like Charlie and me. I don't see anybody telling us to stay up on our mountain. Just the opposite. So I don't see the difference. And you shouldn't, either."

He could feel Dana's astonishment behind him. And why shouldn't she be amazed? He was shocked himself. He'd told himself to ease into this project, to take it slow and not get carried away. Carried away was exactly the words he'd use to describe the speech he'd just made. Still, he couldn't bring himself to regret one word of it.

"I'm voting yes," Bart declared. "I'm not even on the zoning committee and I'm voting yes." In fact, it wouldn't come to a public vote. Or at least, it ought not to. Mason wouldn't put it past Nicholson to try something underhanded like a public referendum to stop the project if the committee gave its approval.

"Thanks, Bart." Mason shook the man's hand. Dana came down the stairs to stand beside him, and together they answered a smattering of questions as the gathering dispersed.

Only when just about everyone had left did he turn to catch Dana staring at him. Unbelief mixed in her eyes with the most alluring delight. He'd just made her very happy. Was that really a surprise? He felt lighter—and yes, happier—than he had in months. As if the clouds had lifted off his life the way they lifted over the mountains after a storm.

He wanted to be alone with her, to try and put into words what had just happened. Even though he wasn't sure he'd ever find the words. But there were just so many people around. So many eyes. And wagging tongues. Maybe that was God protecting him from the unchecked impulses bumping around his chest right now.

Dana walked up to him, face flushed. She tucked a strand of hair behind her ear and glanced down before returning her gaze to him. "Wow," she said. "I mean, wow."

"Um… I hadn't planned on that," he admitted.

"You're pretty compelling on impulse," she said with a small, anxious laugh. "Imagine if you gave it a little forethought?"

Mason looked around, feeling awkward. He sat down on the stairs, needing to feel less on display. "I'm not sure I could make that happen again."

She sat down beside him, casting his memory back to them sitting beside the pond. The place where he first realized what she'd done to change his life even after he tried so hard to shut her out. "How *did* that happen?"

"Arthur Nicholson, if you can believe it. He laid into the project as if it would contaminate the town, and when I realized he could have been talking about Charlie, something just sort of…caught fire." Mason shook his head. "Everything sunk into place all at once, and there was no going back."

"Yeah," she said, laughing nervously again, "You are fully committed now." She softened her voice and turned to look at him. "Are you sure?"

Mason waited for a hesitation, a doubt that never came. "Yes." The word had a perfect solidness to it. When was the last time he'd been this sure about anything?

"Thank you."

Mason felt the warmth of her two words hum through to his bones. "Oh, I'd say we're even."

"We're not just even, we're partners. I rather like the sound of that." She held out her hand for a dramatic handshake.

He took her hand and shook it. But so much of him wanted to keep holding on.

Chapter Thirteen

Mason and Bart put the last of the folding chairs from the breakfast away in the church basement. "You've done good today," the older man said with a hand clamped on Mason's shoulder. "Am I allowed to say it's good to see the old Mason back? I've missed him."

More than one person had said much the same thing since his impassioned speech at the gazebo. Had he been that lifeless in the years since Melony's death? He'd certainly felt lifeless—it was alarming to realize how much of it showed on the outside. "Yeah, you can," he said. "I sort of surprised myself," he admitted.

Bart pushed the closet door shut. "A good cause'll do that to you." His eye took on a mischievous twinkle. "A few other things will do that as well."

"Huh?"

"Certain people."

Mason picked his jacket up from a nearby table. The morning had started off with a bit of a chill while they were setting up but had blossomed into a warm and clear day near-perfect for the breakfast. As if God Himself were placing His stamp of approval on the idea of Camp True North Springs. "Well, I have to admit Art Nicholson riled me up. That man sure has a talent for looking down his nose at people."

Bart chuckled softly. "He does, and if he riled you up, then that'll be the first time I've ever been thankful for his arrogant nature." They started walking toward the main part of the church. "But that's not what I meant."

Mason stopped walking. "What?"

Bart turned to look at him. The man's face was warm and understanding. "Dana."

Mason forced his face to stay neutral, but inside he felt like Charlie caught eating extra cookies. "What?" he repeated, fearful of the answer he could sense coming.

"Come on now. I'm not so old that I can't recognize some things when I see them."

Mason looked both ways down the hallway, then leaned against the wall. "I...no...it's not..." His skin prickled from the exposure of someone else knowing the war going on inside him. Could everyone see it? He wasn't ready for anyone to know. He was still trying to ignore it himself.

"Her, too," Bart said, his face entirely too kind and amused. "But I expect you know that."

"No, I don't." That was mostly true. He'd convinced himself the soft glow coming off her was just his imagination. But if Bart saw it—somehow that made the whole thing that much harder to get his head around. "Where's Charlie?" That was a surefire way to cut this conversation short.

"With Dana and Rita in the church kitchen. Relax a minute." He motioned to the door that led outside to the church's little courtyard. "Walk with me." It was half request, half "don't try to weasel out of this conversation" command.

Mason had little choice but to follow Bart out to the sunny flagstone bench that sat amidst carefully tended succulents and a pretty little fountain. A fountain. These days Mason couldn't see one without thinking of Dana.

They sat down. "Don't you think we all like the idea of you being happy again? Brother, you have been through so much sadness. You deserve a double dose of happiness."

There seemed little hope of hiding it. "I'm not ready. And with the camp project, it all seems…" Mason let his words fall off, and merely waved his hand in a vague gesture of worry.

"And Charlie. I think you are wise to be careful. But don't be so careful that you are foolish. This is a very good thing. For each of you. And who is ever ready for something so big to come into their lives? We wouldn't depend so much on God if we thought we could do it all alone, would we?"

Even with all the confidence Mason felt coursing through him from earlier, it felt as if God was going to have to show up in epic ways for Camp True North Springs to come into being. Especially with the likes of Nicholson flexing his civic muscles against it. "So much could go wrong. We were just getting our feet underneath us, Charlie and I."

Bart gave Mason a very fatherly look. "I hope you'll

forgive me for telling you today was the first time I saw *your* feet underneath *you*. You've been staying out of sight and stumbling for too long. I liked the man I saw today. I've missed him. Seems to me there is so much that could go right." After a pause, he continued, "Forget the big project for a moment. What is your heart telling you?"

Mason opted for total honesty. "My heart is yelling nonsense at me. And I feel guilty for listening." That sounded ridiculous, but he couldn't think of any other way to describe it.

Bart laughed. "Hearts are good at that. And Charlie? What does Charlie think of Dana? I mean, the little pond is an amazing thing, don't you think?"

Word had gotten out about Franco and his pond. Mason knew that wasn't at all the reason Dana did what she did, but the kind act seemed to endear her to many people in North Springs. He saw evidence of that in how they listened this morning. "They've connected, those two. I can't really explain it. But don't you see? I can't risk that friendship. The camp will stretch it enough as it is—Charlie thinks of it as all fun and games now, but when the building starts and the arguments happen and the people show up…if it all goes wrong, he'll blame her," Mason sighed. "And me."

"Charlie needs to see that life goes on. And that risks are worth taking. The world has taken a lot from him. Now you have someone standing in front of you helping you find a way to put it back. And not just for him, but for lots of kids like him. I can't think of a better thing to teach your son, can you?"

When Mason looked away, his chest too full of a dozen different emotions, Bart stood up. "Did you know Rita was not my first wife?"

Mason stood up to meet the man's gaze. "You never told me."

"I should have. But I don't talk about Estella to hardly anyone. We were young and very much in love. She died in a flood. I was young and torn to pieces by it. Lost—like you—for years, thinking that was it. I'd had the love of my life and you don't get two of those."

Bart put his big arm around Mason's shoulder. "But sometimes you do. God sent me Rita. And you know how stubborn that woman is. She had to work hard and fight to get me to see we were meant to be together. I have never been so grateful to lose an argument in my life." He gave Mason's shoulder a squeeze. "You are smarter than me. Maybe don't make Dana fight so hard to see what I already know you see."

"Does Rita know you meddle this much?" Mason asked, feeling young and foolish.

Bart laughed again. "Who do you think sent me to talk to you?"

Mason gave a little gulp. And here he'd thought Bart was just being helpful. "I thought you said Rita was with Dana and Charlie?"

Bart shrugged. "Well, we thought Dana needed a little talking to, too. Only I think Charlie is ahead of all of us. He told Rita he's going to ask Dana to go to Special Ladies Day at school."

When Charlie had mentioned wanting to ask Dana

something after the breakfast, Mason hadn't for a moment considered it would be that. "Now what do I do?"

"If you are as wise as I think you are, you pray she says 'yes.'"

Charlie pointed up to the beautiful stained glass window that made up the front wall of the church. "It's pretty, isn't it? The colors are even better on church mornings."

Dana was enjoying the pint-sized tour of the church Charlie had chosen to give her after they finished returning supplies to the kitchen. The boy had taken her hand as if it was the most natural thing in the world and led her through the building. His commentary on some things was amusing—the carpet was "too red" and the nursery decorations were "nice but silly."

Their final stop was the fellowship hall, even though it was very close to the kitchen where they'd started. Dana wondered about the circular route until Charlie stood in front of her with a serious look on his face. Evidently, he'd meant to end up here all along. She figured it might be to meet up with Mason and Bart as they finished putting away chairs, but those two were long gone.

"I need to ask you something," Charlie said as he showed her the little stage at the far end of the room.

"Okay."

"I want you to come to Special Ladies Day with me instead of Grandma. It's the thing at school. Grandma's been there before anyways. I want you to come this time. Is that okay?"

Much as Dana wasn't a fan of anything called Special Ladies Day, Charlie's invitation charmed her. It implied that she was special to Charlie, and that went straight to her heart. "That's really nice to ask me. But don't you think your grandmother's feelings will be hurt? You and I can think of something else fun to do together." The ease of that offer touched her. She would be happy to do something fun with Charlie. She'd be happy to do anything with the boy. He was coming to mean so much to her.

"But I really want *you* there. Everybody likes you now."

Dana recalled some of the comments from this morning. "I'm not so sure that's true," she admitted. Still, she treasured Charlie's endorsement.

He caught the change in her tone and looked down at his shoes. "You don't wanna come."

Dana squatted down to place herself in his gaze. "No, no, that's not true. I would truly like to come, Charlie, really I would. But, well, it's not really a nice thing to un-invite someone. I'd feel bad if I were your grandma."

Charlie shrugged. "She's just coming because Mom can't. I know that."

Children are wiser than we ever give them credit for, Dana thought. "That doesn't mean she loves you any less and she wouldn't have fun."

"I'd have more fun with you. I like you—and not just 'cause of Franco. Dad wants you to come, too."

This was news. "You talked to your dad about this?" That would have been her next suggestion.

"No, but he'll say yes. He talks about you a lot. And he smiles when he does. I think he likes you, too. He's not so sad lately. And he comes to stuff. And today? Come on—he gave a big speech and everything about the camp." He raised a small eyebrow as if that should tell Dana all she needed to know.

Clearly, Charlie had noticed the powerful change in his father as much as she had. Dana couldn't think of a safe way to respond to that. Mostly because her own heart was galloping at the idea that Mason might be feeling the same affections growing in her. "I'm really glad he's excited about the camp." It occurred to her she hadn't asked a very important question. "Are you?"

He rolled his eyes. "'Course I am. I get to live in a camp. It'll be a whole lot of fun."

"It'll also be a whole lot of work. New people at lots of times. It might not be as much fun as it sounds. You might not like it." It struck her anew that what she had in mind really would turn Charlie and Mason's life upside down. Maybe that wasn't the fresh restart she thought it was. For her, maybe, but did she have the right to ask that of Mason and his son?

Charlie pressed his lips together. "Are you gonna un-invite us from that?" He sounded heartbroken at the prospect.

Maybe she shouldn't have, but Dana pulled Charlie into a hug. "Of course not." It felt so wonderful, so healing, to feel his small arms wrap around her. He hugged her right back, and it was as if her body had been waiting for that hug for years. Maybe it had. "I'd never un-invite you from the camp. It's your home. We might be changing it, but I'd never, ever take it away from you."

"But somebody said you want to take it from us. I told them that's not true."

Charlie should never think she was trying to buy his house out from underneath them. "It's complicated. But it's more like your dad and I—and you—would be working together. It's important to me that you understand that." A thought occurred to her. She pulled away from Charlie so she could look him in the eyes. "Who said that to you? That I want to take your house from you?"

"Some kids."

Dana wasn't going to press him for names, but anger burned in her throat. What a horrible thing for anyone to say—and she could only guess they'd heard it from their parents. Didn't people listen to Mason's impassioned speech in favor of the camp? Couldn't they hear his support for the project in his words?

She pulled Charlie back into the hug, more tightly this time. "I will never take your home from you, ever. Your home will always be yours. If this all works out, I'll just be lucky enough to spend lots of time there." It was closer to how she felt than she'd admitted to anyone. The land she hoped would become Camp True North Springs really was coming to feel like a home to her. "Don't you listen to those kids—or anyone else who says that. They were just being mean because they didn't understand. You and your dad mean a lot to me, and I'd never do anything to make you sad or make you leave."

"Then you'll come? To the day instead of Grandma?"

Dana wasn't sure why he was connecting the two

events so strongly, but if coming to Special Ladies Day gave him a dose of reassurance, she couldn't bring herself to refuse. "Ask your dad and your grandma if it's okay, and I'll be there if they say yes."

Charlie's smile warmed her to her bones. "I knew you would. Mrs. S said you would, too. She said she thought it was the best idea I'd ever had."

So he'd conferred with Rita Salinas on this? When? Dana wondered why she hadn't felt her ears burning. Her stomach did a small flip at the prospect of being the topic of so many North Springs conversations this morning. Opening Camp True North Springs was going to ask more of her than she realized.

As she looked up to see Mason watching them, Dana had one thought: it was worth it.

Mason practically had to lean against the doorway as he watched Charlie hug Dana tight. The power of the sight shot through him, stealing his breath. Charlie had been the recipient of hundreds of hugs since Melony died, but he'd never seen his son hug back the way he was doing right now. Happily, eyes squinted tight, huge smile on his face.

How had all this happened so quickly? Things were shifting so fast, on such an enormous scale. He was frightened by the speed. By the level of care for her that was surging up within him. But that surge was also exhilarating. *Am I wrong, Lord? Caught up in something just because it's the first time I've felt anything about... anything?* Mason laughed at himself, avoiding saying "anyone" as if God didn't already know.

He was trying to figure out how to respond when Charlie caught sight of him and scrambled out of Dana's arms. "Dad!"

Somehow Charlie's rush into his arms was extra sweet. "Hey there, buddy." He tried—probably without much success—to act as if nothing huge had just happened. "Whatcha doing?"

"Showing Dana around and asking her to come to Special Ladies Day."

Dana offered a worried look over Charlie's head, cringing at the bold invitation she clearly knew was displacing Mason's mom. "I…" she began.

"She already said yes," Charlie cut in, his chin tipping up with the victory.

"I *said* you needed to talk to your dad and your grandmother, and that it's not nice to un-invite people." Dana's words were polite and appropriate, but Mason could see in her eyes how the invitation had touched her. He could see it in the way she hugged his son, too. He saw the care in her eyes when she looked at Charlie. It radiated off her when Charlie had put his head on her shoulder that incredible day of the little pond and the flowers. It was starting to hum between them whenever they were together.

"It might take a tiny bit of convincing," he replied, "but I think Grandma could be persuaded. After all, we just learned that the three of us make a pretty persuasive team, didn't we?"

"What's 'persuasive' mean?" Charlie asked.

"It's what you just did to Dana. Get her to come around to your way of thinking."

"Dad," Charlie groaned. "She wanted to come all along. I could tell."

Dana's sweet smile said "He's right," even though she didn't offer up a word in reply.

Dana Preston was indeed a special lady. Why not let Charlie celebrate that at the school event?

Chapter Fourteen

Mason gazed across the piles of papers and charts spread out on the dining room table Tuesday night. "We're ready." The zoning committee meeting was the following night. They'd worked with Theo all day Monday to submit their formal request. True to the architect's prediction, Arthur Nicholson had called for an emergency public hearing.

"Do you think we really are?" Dana answered, scanning the pile of papers as well.

"As ready as we'll ever be." Was Mason nervous? Yes. But he was also confident. They had all the ammunition they needed to fight the critics Arthur Nicholson might rouse up.

They also had a battalion of prayer. Rita and Bart had recruited an army of church folk to be in prayer during Wednesday's hearing.

Mason looked at the far end of the dining room, at the wall that would be pushed out to make the current dining room into a dining hall that could seat thirty people. It wasn't hard to envision. He could almost hear the conversations. Parents sharing the experience of a family torn by grief. Children hearing how other kids really knew how they felt. Out of nowhere his mind brought up an image—a daydream, really—of a slightly older Charlie talking to a young boy saying, "It gets better. You'll be all right."

He blinked and swallowed hard, moved by the imaginary vision of his son so healed and healthy. That Charlie, that possible future for Charlie, was worth any amount of work.

Dana touched his elbow. "You okay?" She'd given him several little casual touches since the day of the breakfast. He'd noticed and vividly remembered all of them.

"Yeah," he managed to say. He hadn't figured out a way to talk to Dana about it, but each of those small touches told him she knew. Not only had he changed, *they* had changed. Or were changing. Into what? The possible answer filled him with equal parts wonder and fear. The care unfurling in his heart—it was startling. Brilliant and frightening. He hadn't counted on returning to life putting so much at stake.

"I never got a chance to tell you how amazing you were on Saturday." Her voice was tentative, as if she wanted to tell him but knew, as he did, that these were dangerous waters in which to wade. The attraction building up between them refused to be ignored, no matter how sensible a choice that was. "I'm not sure we'd be so ready if you hadn't been so…persuasive." The word had become an inside joke between them, a touchstone of sorts. Or maybe just a code word for the growing closeness neither of them felt ready to name.

"You were pretty amazing yourself. Those stories. It made things real for people." He chose not to tamp down his admiration tonight. His affection he'd hold in check. But his admiration? She deserved to know how he felt about what she'd done.

"I just told people what I'd seen."

Could she really not see how she'd affected people? "No, it was way more than that. You took the idea of Camp True North Springs and told us what it could do in actual lives. The holes it could fill. Nobody else could have done that. Nobody's been through what you've been through."

"You have. We've both seen what those kinds of wounds look like."

Her face flushed—a very un-Dana-like thing he found he enjoyed very much. Mason wondered if she realized that by stopping her onslaught of persuasion to him, by dropping her warrior shield a little bit more each day, she had won him over. Totally. He'd been so sure he'd never care for another woman again. Guys like him just didn't get that kind of second chance. And yet feelings were there. New, unsteady…and probably the worst possible idea right at this moment. But there, nonetheless.

"And you and Charlie have been through so much more," she went on. "The loss. I can come up with all the ideas in the world and it won't match the power of someone who knows. I've only been close to it. Seen the start of it and the fallout. You've really been through it."

Mason leaned against the table, wanting to say a whole bunch of things but worried all of them would take them places they ought not to go. "I never could make sense of it. I mean, how could I? Melony's death was so senseless." He swept his hands across the documents. "If this comes out of it, it'll make just a little bit of sense. Like the whole thing won't have been a colossal, pointless tragedy. That helps, you know?" Redeemed seemed like such a fancy term for what he felt, even though that's what Pastor Gorman kept calling the idea of the camp. "The whole 'all things work together for good' business from the Bible."

"Yeah, that." There was such a compelling warmth in her eyes. How had he ever thought them cool and harsh?

Mason suddenly had to know. "Do you believe in that? In God's ability to work everything—even what happened to you and to me—for good?" All the affection he might feel for her couldn't be the only foundation for this. He had to know she felt God's hand in the camp as strongly as he did. In her life as strongly as he'd clung to the knowledge of God's hand in his life.

The look she gave him was honest. "I'm coming to. I...want to." She gave a small sigh. "Hard not to with the way things have lined up, isn't it?"

Mason let himself hold her gaze longer than he should have. Her eyes had a way of making him feel all kinds of things were possible.

"Is wanting to enough?" she asked. "I've never had... what you have. That kind of rock-steady faith."

Mason almost laughed. "Rock steady? It's never been rock steady. More like shaky, scary, hanging on by your fingernails. So if you want to talk about wanting more faith, I'm right there beside you."

It was a dangerous choice of words. Something new glowed in her eyes that made him want to be a braver man. A less wounded man.

"We make a pretty good team," she offered. Mason couldn't tell if she were saying more, or it was him just wishing she were.

"We make an awesome team," came Charlie's declaration as he burst into the room from his mission of putting on pajamas up in his room. He hopped up on one of the dining room chairs and surveyed the documents like a king approving battle plans. "I don't get why I can't be there. I'm part of the team."

"You definitely are," Mason said, only half-grateful for the distraction to pull his thoughts back to more sensible topics. "But you are the part of the team that has to be in bed long before Wednesday night's boring adult meeting will be over." That was only half-true. The meeting might indeed run long, but Mason was more worried about it running hot—heated arguments hot—and didn't want Charlie to be in the audience for that. He'd thought it wise to arrange for a sitter.

Dana began gathering up the papers. "We all should get a good night's sleep. Thanks for the really good tacos, Mason."

He liked the way she said his name. It stuck in his ear like a happy tune.

"I helped," Charlie added.

"Thanks for your help with the really good tacos, Charlie. You give Nicco a run for his money."

Charlie's eyes sparkled at the compliment. "Don't tell him that. He'll be mad." He hopped off the chair and promptly wrapped his arms around Dana's waist, a ball of shameless affection in superhero jammies. "G'night."

He'd hugged Dana each time they'd been together since the pancake breakfast. Each time, Mason could watch the embrace wash over her, filling her features with care and wonder. Charlie was such a gift to the world, to him. Maybe this broken little family wasn't so battered that it couldn't put some good back into the world. Maybe all of it really could work together for good. God, working a wonder through the pushy woman he'd tried to throw off his land not so long ago.

"Good night, you," Dana said. Mason wondered if Charlie could hear all the emotion in Dana's voice that he could. "See you Friday."

Friday was Special Ladies Day. Would they be celebrating a victory that night? Or recuperating from a stinging defeat?

A town zoning committee meeting should be nothing to a woman who has stared down the gun barrel of an angry gang member. Sheer logic should have told Dana her anxiety level was way beyond the situation. But nothing about this entire journey had much to do with logic.

She and Mason stood on the sidewalk outside of the town hall Wednesday evening, getting ready to go into the meeting that was scheduled to start in a few minutes. He was trying to act calm and confident, but she could read his true feelings. Tonight meant as much to him as it did to her, and that knowledge lodged itself deep inside.

Mason fished in his jacket pocket. "I'm not one for tokens, but Charlie said to give you this." He pulled out a smooth, round pebble. "It's from our first trip to Hawaii. Charlie brings it with him when he's worried. Melony told him to rub his fingers over it and remember how old the world is. Kind of helps put things in perspective—which is better than luck as far as I'm concerned."

Dana took it. It was warm from Mason's hand. She passed her fingers over the smooth dark surface and pulled in a steady breath.

His gaze was reassuring. "The thing about faith is that you can *know*—even when you can't *feel*—that things will turn out. I've known for a long time, but lately is the first time I've felt it in a long time. So even if tonight doesn't turn out the way we hoped, I want to thank you for that."

Mason's words went straight to her heart. Despite what he'd just said, how could she bear failing him if this didn't work? How cruel would it be to pull him into this project, care for his son—and for him—the way she did, and have it come to nothing? Arthur Nicholson was wrong. Camp True North Springs could not be anywhere else but on Mason's land. It was meant to be in North Springs. Ordained. She could believe that now, stake her ground on the fragile faith that seemed to be unfolding in her like the ripples on Charlie's little pond.

"I said prayers for us tonight." A simple statement, huge in meaning. Dana wanted Mason to know how much all this had changed her, even if she couldn't put it together as eloquently as he just had.

The words lit a glow in his eyes. "I'm glad to hear that."

Dana lost her nerve. "Well, me and a lot of people, I know. Rita's got a whole army in there and everywhere."

Mason wouldn't let her back down from her earlier statement. "True, but I'm especially glad to hear you prayed. We can't do this without it, you know. Take it from a guy who's been trying to do without it for way too long."

He took her hand that held the stone, and then reached to her other hand to place it on top, palm to palm. Like a prayer. Then he placed each of his hands over hers. Dana felt the gesture radiate through her— tender and holy and caring and calming. Scar tissue was pale and tough without sensation. Dana felt at that moment as if the scar tissue fell off her soul. Something rosy and tender and with a million strong feelings came forth from underneath. It made her unsteady and stole her breath. Tonight *had* to go their way. She had to be able to push the plans through, to give this to Mason and Charlie—and to herself. Dana couldn't even begin to survive the consequences if it didn't. Despite barely knowing how, she'd poured her heart into her prayers. If God knew her the way Mason seemed to think He did, then He'd know how much she needed this.

"Time to go be persuasive," she said, her voice thick with the emotion of the moment.

She and Mason pushed through the doors to the little auditorium on the bottom floor of the town hall where such meetings were held. Dana was stunned at the number of people in the room. Were they all here to support Camp True North Springs? Or were they all here to object? She recognized many of the faces, but there were still scores of people in North Springs she hadn't met.

It wasn't a comforting sight to see Arthur Nicholson in the center chair on the dais at the front of the room. Dana knew a battle face when she saw one. The gavel in his hand came down with the ferocity of a weapon as she took her place beside Mason in the front row. Theo sat two seats away. Dana held the pebble tight in her hand as she heard Mason pull in a deep breath.

Arthur cleared his throat loudly. "This specially convened meeting will now come to order. We have a single item on the agenda, that being the zoning reclassification of the land parcel commonly known as the land of Mason Avery. The petition before the committee is to rezone this parcel from residential to a commercial recreational facility."

Did he have to be so formal in his wording? Or was he trying to intimidate the room? She was used to people whose language went south in a conflict, not highhanded. *What am I doing here? This isn't what I know. Why did I think I could do this?* All her confidence seemed to leave her in the wake of Arthur's glare.

Mason was as passionate in his presentation as he had been at the pancake breakfast. His arguments had to be their best tactics—it was his land, his family's land, after all. Dana took encouragement from the small comments of "Yes!" and "Wonderful plans!" from the audience...until Arthur slammed his gavel again and told the crowd to keep quiet.

"There will be order in this proceeding or I will clear the room," he boomed.

When the time came for Dana to give her presentation, she rose with all the conviction she could. Still, her words fell short of the solid feeling her stories had at the breakfast.

"How can you assure me you're not bringing criminals to that land?" one woman asked in a loud voice when it came time for public commentary. "You can't tell me violence doesn't happen to those kind of people more than anyone else. Why would we invite people like that here?"

"This is not a rehabilitation program," Dana tried to respond with calm facts. "The people coming here would be victims. Families who have lost a member to violence. This would be like inviting someone you know who had been through a hard time to come for a visit."

"No, it wouldn't. We don't know these people," said a man Dana recognized as the owner of a real estate office in town. She'd come to him looking for a home when her rental at Marion's was done. He'd been friendly then, but the harsh tone of his words now surprised and stung her. "They're total strangers," he went on, pointing at her. "You said yourself at the gazebo some of these kids react with violence because that's all they've ever known. We don't want that here."

Mason had been right to ensure Charlie heard none of this. She was having trouble holding it together as a grown woman. She had no training to prepare her for this, and it felt so much larger than the changing of a few numbers on a zoning document.

"I can't believe what I'm hearing from my own neighbors," Nicco Guerro said. "I would have given anything for an opportunity like this when I was young and stupid. It would have changed my life."

Half the room nodded in agreement, while another half seemed to think Nicco's words made the perfect argument against Camp True North Springs. It went on like that for over an hour, with praise and hope going head to head with criticism and fear.

Dana was almost glad Arthur refused to extend the stated time period for public commentary. The tension in the room was mounting. When Arthur called for the commission vote, Dana couldn't begin to say which way it would go. Where was God's provision, where was the fortress of prayer all those kind people had said they were building around Mason and Charlie? She felt unarmed, vulnerable, even foolish. So much of her wanted to reach out and grab Mason's hand for support as Arthur called the names of each commission member asking for their vote.

She blinked hard as the votes came in four to three.

Against the zoning that would allow for Camp True North Springs.

They'd been denied.

Chapter Fifteen

Mason couldn't believe it. He'd known there were people who had misgivings about the camp, but what he heard tonight went so much further than that. What had Arthur Nicholson told these people? It couldn't have been anything based on facts—nothing in the plans they presented tonight or ahead of time warranted what he'd just seen.

Had tonight been a civilized discussion, an actual debate about facts and options, he might have been able to swallow the outcome.

But tonight had been about fear. Fear that somehow the people who had known the worst of what life had to offer must actually *be* the worst people life had to offer. And that was him, wasn't it? Didn't he—and Charlie, for that matter—fit the profile these people were trying to keep away from North Springs? It was as if he'd somehow managed to hold a mirror up to the town, forcing them to admit that troubled kids could be anywhere, that violence picked all kinds of victims. Only they refused to see and hated him for trying to show them.

My neighbors. My neighbors. The two words pounded in his thoughts over and over. Mason had lived here his whole life, grown up with half the people in this room. He thought he knew these people, thought these people knew him. Truth be told, half the room *did* support him, made encouraging comments and went out of their way to show how glad they were at his return to town. But the other half…

All of Dana's earlier nervousness had left her. Now she stood very still, a warrior glare trained on Arthur Nicholson. The woman beside him radiated combat—a woman he could easily believe had faced down hardened criminals. His first thought was that he had to get her out of this room before she let her rage get the better of her. Falling back and living to fight another day was the only option here, and Mason wasn't sure Dana had fall back in her vocabulary now, if ever.

He tugged her arm. "Dana, let's go."

"These people are your neighbors," she gasped as she yanked her arm back out of his grasp. It made Mason wonder if he'd voiced his earlier thoughts without realizing it. She flung the arm in Arthur's direction. "Your *friends*. He talked like you were throwing the town off a cliff."

"I don't get how he did it," Theo said, shaking his head in astonishment. "He must have spent every hour since the breakfast pitting people against you. I didn't think he'd get to the committee like that."

"He got to the crowd, and the crowd got to the committee," Mason muttered. Whether or not it was true, Mason felt personally broadsided by the opposition. As if they were against *him*, not just what he was trying to do. What he and Dana were trying to do. If someone had asked him three hours ago if he loved North Springs, he'd have said yes. He'd kept to himself lately and kept the town at a distance, but it was still his home. His father's home. His grandfather's home.

Now? The betrayal was so sharp and fresh he didn't know what to feel. Were it not for Charlie, Mason couldn't rightly say he wouldn't point his truck out of town right now and keep driving. The words he'd heard hurled at him tonight would never leave him. He could never, ever remember feeling about North Springs the way he did right now. Why on earth had God led him down this incredible path, only to meet with what he'd seen tonight?

The one and only blessing—and slim blessing it was at that—was his choice to leave Charlie at home. Mason hoped his son would never hear what had been said tonight. "How am I going to tell Charlie?" he said as much to himself as everyone in the room.

The look on Dana's face at that question sliced through Mason's heart. No one answered the question because there was no answer. No way to tell a little boy how fear had turned his neighbors ugly. And that was the word for it: ugly.

"We'll appeal." Theo's declaration was angry and urgent. "We can do that."

The huff Dana gave in response voiced all the doubt Mason currently felt. There seemed little hope now that Nicholson had ignited such opposition to Camp True North Springs. The name felt darkly ironic now: North

Springs had shown its *true* colors tonight. Mason was heartsick at what he'd seen. He was beyond tempted to just throw his hands up and walk away. When he met some of these people on the square tomorrow—if he dared to venture into town, that is—Mason couldn't predict what he'd say. Actually, he could, and it wasn't anything Charlie should ever hear.

"It's not over," Theo insisted.

"Of course it's not over," Bart said, coming up to clasp Mason's arm. "We won't let it be over."

"How?" Dana asked, futility drawing the one word sharp and tight.

Bart drew in a deep breath. "Well, I don't know that yet. But we will figure it out. I don't want that man to have the last word on this." Bart furrowed his eyebrows and threw Arthur a dark look.

Paul Summers walked by. Up until last night Mason had completely forgotten Nathan's father sat on the zoning committee. "Sorry things didn't go your way." He didn't sound like he was sorry one bit. "It's just not a project for a town like ours." He had said "ours," but Mason could hear the "mine" Paul was surely thinking. *You're not going to put something like that in* my *town.*

"Funny," Mason let himself fire back, "I thought it was exactly the kind of project a town like *mine* should have."

"I doubt your dad would have seen it that way. There are other ways to save your land, Mason. Not this."

Paul could not have struck a lower blow. It stomped on the raw nerve of Mason's recent lean years. The man in front of him could not possibly know the struggle to survive under the weight of Mason's loss. How easy it was to judge from the comfort of his shiny, happy family. Ashamed as he was of it, Mason understood the brutal urge to throw something that had been Charlie's undoing two weeks ago.

Nicco's grip came on his hand, one Mason hadn't even realized he'd balled into a fist. "Not worth it, *amigo*. Stand down." Nicco stepped between Mason and Paul. "Good night, Paul. Go home and see if you can sleep easy after what happened here tonight."

Mason felt as if it would be years before he could sleep easy again. Numb was so much better than the whiplash of rage coursing through his body right now. It was like being yanked back to the injustice of Melony's accident all over again. A wickedly unfair world had him in its crosshairs, shooting down any hopes for happiness.

Dana was packing up her battalion of file folders as if she were picking up bodies on a battlefield. He ought to talk to her, talk with her about the defeat they'd suffered, but how? What was there to say? "Dana…" he managed to blurt out.

"Don't," she said, her eyes still wide in shock. "I need to get out of here. Now."

She was right. Even in his own distress he could see that she was strung so tight if anyone said the wrong thing to her, it would be disastrous. "I'll come over later," he said, not caring who thought what about how that sounded. He needed to sort out the aftermath of this with her, not alone, and knew she needed the same. The only way through this was with each other.

"No," she said even as he could see an overwhelming loneliness in her eyes. "I… Don't."

Some part of him thought walking her to her house would be the polite thing to do, but who was he kidding? Dana was a police officer. She trained to protect and defend.

Not from this, he thought to himself as he watched her push through the lingering crowd to get out of the auditorium. *Not from anything like this*.

Dana was glad Marion's house was close enough to the square that she had walked tonight. Driving anywhere—except maybe clear out of town—felt beyond her. She stomped at high speed across the square toward the house, her tote bag of carefully organized files whacking against her chest as she clutched it. The air stretched too thin, and the moonlight washed sharp and harsh through the clear summer night.

She cut across the grass past the quaint gazebo. Had it only been four days since she felt confident telling her stories, gaining momentum as the town seemed to embrace the idea she'd brought? All that charm felt like a false veneer as she dashed past the circular structure. North Spring's pretty shell was just that—a shell. And now it seemed everyone feared she was here to crack that shell. Some rule of perfection existed, and she had violated it in coming here with the idea she had. It was on her. She'd done that.

Dana had faced horrific confrontations, urban battles with guns drawn and murderous shouts, and not felt the fog of dread that seemed to cloud her thoughts now. The sense of personal failure was something new and unmanageable. Only one thought came sharp and clear in all the noise clanging everywhere in her mind: *I've ruined it. I've ruined it for Mason and Charlie.*

She'd started a war. Truly, that's what it felt like. To sit in that room and watch people she knew claimed to be neighbors say horrible, mean-spirited things to each other and to Mason? When the opponents hadn't shown up at the breakfast—and then again, why would they?— she'd made the terrible mistake of assuming they didn't exist. That only Arthur was their adversary. Tonight had shown how wrong she was.

It wasn't hard to guess how things would go from here. Mason's face told it all. He wouldn't fight it. There was no hope of finding a way through the conflict she'd seen tonight. No, he would retreat back up the mountain and stay there. All the financial challenges would continue to mount. Someday—all too soon— he would throw up his hands and surrender to them. Charlie would slide further into his emotional valley, finding new ways to grow into an angry soul. People would reach out to the two of them the way they'd been reaching out since Melony died, and their efforts would fall on deaf ears.

Dana fought back the tears as she thrust her key into the house's front door, grunting when it battled back. It seemed a particular torture that she was locking herself in a house full of fragile objects. So much of her wanted to yell and thrash and pound things.

She tossed the bag of files onto the only safe place in the house: the kitchen table. The pile slid a bit from the force of her toss, knocking the hymnal onto the floor. It seemed a fitting symbol for the utter lack of victory tonight had been. She left it lying on the tiles, despite how disrespectful it felt.

Charlie. Dana's heart broke at the thought of how this would hit him. He deserved to see Camp True North Springs come to life in front of his eyes. He deserved to see the good of Franco's little pond ripple out into the large-scale good that the camp would have been. *Would have been*. It would be hard to find three sadder words in the world tonight. Could those four committee members have voted the way they had if Charlie were in front of them? Nicco's words to Paul Summers echoed in her ears: "Go home and see if you can sleep easy after what happened here tonight."

Her phone rang in her coat pocket as she headed toward the bedroom. She didn't even look at it. She wanted to fall onto the bed and yell into the fussy mountain of pillows Marion piled on the bed. Scream her anger and disappointment into the mounds of fringe and ruffles. She dropped her coat thoughtlessly at the bedroom door and let her knees buckle to bring her to the floor next to the bed. It was too much effort to climb onto the high mattress. Down on the floor felt where she ought to be. Dana pulled her knees up, let her head fall onto them, and cried. Hard. And long.

You knew it could end this way, she lectured herself. *This was a wild risk from the beginning. You let yourself forget that.* Trouble was, this wasn't a case of things going back to the way things were. There was no going back. Years of witnessing conflict told her there'd be no healing the divide that split open in town tonight. At least not for Mason, perhaps not for anyone. She'd started to believe the lie that she could help to heal him, maybe had even been sent here to heal him, and had only succeeded in deepening his wounds.

"I'm sorry," she wailed to the empty dark room. "I'm so, so sorry." She grabbed one of the pillows leaning off the mattress above her, a velvety maroon rectangle with gigantic tassels on every corner. She held it to her chest as she let the tears come again. This burned worse than the bullets, cut more than the surgeon's knife, ached more deeply than the long weeks of recovery. Before, she had lost the ability to be a mother. And that was awful, wrenching. Now, she'd lost hope of ever making a difference. And there didn't seem to be anything more awful than that.

What now, God? It was more of a soul cry than any kind of prayer. A desperate plea for wisdom she surely didn't have. *You're going to have to show me where to go from here.*

At some point she must have fallen asleep because the chime of an email message woke her from a fitful doze. She fumbled for her coat on the floor across the room, reaching into the pocket as the device chimed again. She'd meant to simply shut it off, but managed to see the notifications for two voice mails and a pair of texts from Mason. Dana squinted her eyes shut. She couldn't. It'd hurt too much to hear how he was feeling, how much he must resent the attack he'd received tonight. She put the phone back down on the ground, face down. Unable to look, but unable to go so far as to turn it off.

A second chime came five minutes later, one for a text this time. Maybe there was no avoiding this. Pulling in a deep breath, Dana turned the phone over and tapped the icon to bring up text messages. There were two from Mason, yes, but there was another text, a more recent one: You have received a high-priority email from Anthony Derrick. Captain Derrick?

Dana almost laughed. Captain Derrick's high-priority emails were a standing joke in the department. To Derrick, every email was a high priority. The man wrote dozens of them, all long and many of them unnecessary. Why was she still getting one of those—or more precisely, why this one?

Curiosity—or the impulse to avoid reading or listening to anything from Mason right now—got the better of her. For no good reason, Dana pulled up the email on her phone. Maybe it was a long description of some required paperwork she no longer had to submit. Maybe it was photos from the department cookout she'd missed back in Denver.

It wasn't any of those things. It was one of Derrick's long emails, to be sure. Dana skimmed it, sure her sadness was clouding her thinking because it read like the last thing she'd expected.

She sucked in her breath at the last sentence, sitting on its own at the bottom of three long and wordy paragraphs: There's a spot waiting for you if you're ready to come home.

Chapter Sixteen

Come home?

The words no longer made sense. Somehow in the past few weeks Denver had stopped being home. This odd, figurine-filled little house that belonged to someone else had somehow become more like home than any apartment she'd ever had in Denver. Almost all her things were stuffed in Marion's garage and still this little house on the town square felt like home.

More than any of that, the house on the side of the mountain, the one with the silly little pond and ceramic frog, felt like home.

Come home? No. Run back to Denver? Retreat back to Denver, actually. Hadn't she prayed for God's wisdom on what to do next before she fell asleep? Was He showing her? Sometimes retreat really was the only safe way to live to fight another day.

Derrick would take her back in a heartbeat. He'd been so reluctant to let her leave in the first place. She had old colleagues back there, like Sawyer Bradshaw, who were still friends. Why leave that? And really, who was she kidding? This never would have worked. She had no credentials other than her own experience and persistence. Even if she somehow managed to buy the land, to overthrow Nicholson and his army of naysayers, she needed materials and counselors and psychologists and a bunch of other skilled people.

How had she ever kidded herself this could work? When had she become the kind of person to buy into such a pipe dream? Dana couldn't tell if her abdomen ached from fatigue, from injury or from sorrow. Did it really matter? She hugged the pillow to her midsection and sat on the floor waiting for the agony to go away.

She wasn't sure how much time had passed when the carousel melody of Marion's doorbell pierced the darkness of the house. She heard pounding on the door, and a voice she recognized as Mason's calling her name. Her eyes squinted shut at the realization. How could she face him? How could she look at him knowing she'd pulled and pulled and dragged him into this project only to meet with what had happened tonight?

"Dana, let me in." Mason's voice was pained and tired.

She dragged herself downstairs and to the door. Pulling it open felt as if it took superhuman effort. Every inch of her ached, most especially her heart. And if it wasn't already broken, Mason's face crushed what was left of her heart. "I'm… I…" She needed a hundred ways to say I'm sorry and couldn't even find the words for one.

He said nothing. He simply closed the space between

them and pulled her into his arms. The moment defied description, a flood of emotion and regret and raw disappointment combined with aching wonder of being held by him. Because she had, in fact, been aching to be held by him. She, the battle-hardened warrior, the tough-love mother figure to some of the force's fiercest officers, just wanted to be held. It didn't matter that it was the man she'd wounded, the man whose life she'd upended for her own misguided Pollyanna dream.

"I'm sorry," she wept into his shoulder. "I should never have come here. I came for all the wrong reasons." Suddenly a flood of words gushed out of her. "It's *your* land, it's *your* family, this is *your* town and I just came here and…"

Mason pulled back. "And changed *everything*." He gave the word an emphasis she didn't deserve.

"For the worse," she insisted.

He offered a defeated shrug. "Feels like it at the moment." He smoothed back a lock of her hair. "I'm not sorry."

"How can you say that? The things people said…" They'd stopped just short of accusing him of selling out the town to a shady cause in order to save his own skin. Someone had even used the word "contaminate." How could he look at some of these people as neighbors ever again?

She should step back from his embrace, but she couldn't bring herself to it. It felt as if his arms were the only thing holding her upright, the only thing keeping her whole self from falling to dust.

"I'm not sorry," he repeated. "It's not turned out anything close to how I wanted. How I expected, even. But I can't say I'm sorry that you're...here. That you're in my life. In Charlie's life."

Mason held her gaze, and Dana's legs felt unsteady beneath her for a whole different reason. It seemed impossible to her that he could feel what she felt, what she saw reflected in his eyes. She had to be wrong, had to be seeing only what she wanted to see. "Mason..." she began, but couldn't find a way to say more. She'd come here to find a way to make a difference, and all she'd done was make a mess. A terrible, ugly mess for two people she'd come to care so much about.

"I'll admit, this is hard." His tone was weary and disappointed, but he still did not release his arms from around her. She couldn't make sense of it.

"But my life's been only an empty kind of hard for way too long," he went on. "Tonight was the first time in a long time I drove down that mountain *wanting* to be in town. Wanting to be part of life again. I was ready to fight for this wild idea. An idea the pushiest woman I've ever met kept insisting I had to be part of."

Mason kept touching her hair. So softly. Dana thought if he touched her cheek with that much tenderness she might melt on the spot. Her, melting. Who could have ever seen this coming?

"I'm not ready to let that go," Mason continued. "No matter how ugly this gets. I'm not ready to let *you* go. And I'm sure Charlie isn't either. The camp's not dead, it's just hit a snag."

Dana could almost laugh at that. What had happened

tonight was a full-scale assault of opposition, not a snag. "How can you say that?"

And then he did touch her cheek, and Dana's eyes fluttered closed at the power of it. Is this what people meant when they said *swoon*?

"Because this is about so much more than land. Or a camp. This is about…this." Mason leaned in and touched his lips to hers with such a gentle kiss that *swoon* most definitely was the only word that applied.

Dana tried to say his name, but it only came out as something awkward between a squeak and a sigh. She ought to be more composed, but it was hopeless. Too many emotions rushed through her.

Mason pulled back, looking at her with the tenderest question in his eyes. "Okay?" he asked. As if he'd done something wrong. As if he hadn't done the thing she'd been wishing for but didn't feel she deserved. She'd convinced herself she needed to give him the camp to gain his heart. Would he really give it to her even if they failed? Could it be that he'd need it more *because* they failed?

Dana managed a bumbled, astonished nod. She put her hand to his chest and felt his heart race beneath her palm. A tiny bit of her brave self showed up out of all the weariness and she let herself take in the warmth of his gaze. The brilliance of his dark eyes and the strength of the arms around her. A bit more of the bravery returned, and Dana leaned in to return his kiss. Maybe not quite as gently as he kissed her.

The world and all its worries faded in the glow of their kiss. She drew strength and joy from it, felt healed despite all the jabs and wounds of what people had said. As if by somehow combining their wounds they made a healed whole. It had been so pointless to resist this, to keep herself from the connection she felt with Mason. The connection she now felt absolutely certain God had designed for her—for them—all along.

Mason pulled away a bit after the long kiss, his eyes gleaming and his smile broad and warm. The power of the moment for him showed on his features, and in the gallop of his heart she could still feel under her palm. "That," he said a little breathlessly, "was even better than I imagined." He let his forehead rest against hers, and Dana let her eyes fall closed at the tenderness of the gesture. She'd known so many men who were strong—relentlessly strong—that it was a wonder to know a man who could be strong and tender at the same time.

Maybe, just maybe, it would be okay to have come to North Springs looking for property and finding the treasure of a partner instead. If her future did not contain Camp True North Springs, perhaps God had other plans for her. Plans she could welcome with Mason by her side.

And, of course Charlie. Without moving from his closeness to her, she heard him whisper, "I have to get back to Charlie. I've only got the sitter for another thirty minutes." He pulled back just enough to catch her gaze. "I *really* wished you'd answered your phone half an hour ago."

She was so pleased to hear the "it's okay now" in his tone of voice. Even though a lot of it was far from okay, this one piece of it made up for all the others.

"I couldn't bear to hear how I'd brought this on you. I'd be so furious. I *am* so furious. Those people. How could they do that?"

"I am furious," he said, running his hand down her arm to take her hands firmly in his. Its echo of the way he'd touched her before the committee meeting reassured her. "At them. But it did wake me up to what was more important. I didn't count on getting angry enough to come over here determined to kiss you." He laughed softly. "And I'm not sure I was counting on you kissing me like that. Wow."

It spread through her, warm and sparkling, to know he felt the same way. "Seriously." She let her thumb wander across the back of his hand, smitten by the fact she could do something so…romantic. "What do we do now?"

Mason sighed. He'd been asking himself that question for hours. "I don't know," he admitted. "Prayer would be a good start." He didn't have another antidote for the sense of betrayal pulling at him. "I'm not much good to anyone in my present state. I don't know how to react to what I heard and saw tonight." He shook his head. "From people I thought I knew." He looked right into her eyes, realizing that so much of his healing seemed to be there. "I'm going to need your help."

Did she feel the same way? Did she feel the only hope she had for healing was beside him? When she said, "Me, too," the steel in his spine eased up a little. She was brave and strong, and he needed to borrow that spirit from her. And not just tonight, but for a long time afterward.

As if she'd realized his need for that warrior spirit, Dana straightened her shoulders a bit. Some of the determination returned to the vivid green of her eyes. "We'll figure this out, the two of us. The three of us, actually."

The three of us. Mason had let himself believe he'd never get to use those words again, that it would always be just him and Charlie against the world. What a gift it was to let the lie of that fall away.

"Charlie means the world to me. You know that, don't you?" She squeezed his hand, and he heard her unspoken, *You mean the world to me.*

There was the most amazing piece of the whole thing: Charlie did mean so much to her. It was one thing to know the attraction and affection he had for her and she for him, but the extra blessing of how close she and Charlie had become astounded him. "I do know it," he said, hoping his words reflected the enormous gratitude he felt. "And he knows it, too."

Mason wanted to stay here and talk to her for hours. To work through this monumental wall thrown up in front of them. To hold her—and have her hold him—until the raw pain of tonight subsided. Instead, he looked at his watch and winced. "I have to go." He kissed her again, far more quickly than he would have liked. "Next time answer your phone right away," he joked, his voice husky.

Dana laughed. "First ring." She brought her hand up to stroke the curve of his jaw, and Mason forgot how to breathe. What a breathtaking woman she was. How had he not seen that from the first second she stood at his gate? Why had it taken him so long to see? "Good night, Mason," she said, delight setting a glow in her eyes.

He let his head fall back and gave a small groan. "That's what did it at first, you know. The way you say my name." It was true. The way she said his name went through him like a roll of thunder. Mason forced himself to pull away, letting go of her hand slowly, down to the fingertips at the very last. "Good night. We'll figure out things in the morning."

"We will." The determination in her voice was a blessing, a benediction. There was a way out of this. They just couldn't see it yet.

But together, they would.

Chapter Seventeen

Charlie did not take the news well.

Mason had expected that and had rehearsed a dozen different ways to tell his son, but none of them could soften the blow with any success.

"Why do we have to have their stupid permission anyways?" Charlie pouted as he dumped a second helping of cereal into his bowl Thursday morning. "This is our house."

Mason wasn't sure there was a useful way to explain zoning ordinances to a seven-year-old. "Certain parts of North Springs are set up for certain things. You wouldn't want an airport to move in next door, right?"

Charlie scowled out the window. "Nobody lives next door to us."

Mason sighed and tried again. "If we became a camp, we'd be changing the rules for this property. You can't just do that without asking."

"But you asked," Charlie insisted. "You said you were following the rules."

There wasn't any way around it. "And people said no."

"Why?" his son whined. Mason had to admit, he felt like whining the same question, even though he knew the answer.

There wasn't really a safe way to explain the fear his neighbors had displayed. "Do you know what violence means?"

Charlie poked his spoon around in his bowl. "Bad stuff. Mean stuff."

"All the people who would come to the camp have had bad stuff or mean stuff happen to them."

"Like us."

Those two words burned into Mason's chest like a firebrand. "Like us. I think the people who said no are afraid of that." He couldn't bring himself to say that some of his own neighbors believed bad things made for bad people. Yes, it was true some of the time, but it was never true all of the time. Nor did it have to be. That was the whole point of Camp True North Springs, wasn't it?

"That's dumb," Charlie declared.

"It is," Mason had to agree. "I hope we can get people to see that. Only I'm not sure how we'll do that just yet. Miss Dana and I—and you—are going to have to figure that out. With some of our friends, I hope."

Charlie pushed his bowl away. "I don't wanna go to Special Ladies Day anymore. I don't wanna go to school today. I don't wanna go anywhere."

Mason could certainly relate to that urge to stay up on the mountain. A month ago, he would have. But he was a different man now, and he was pretty sure that man was going to have to go back down the mountain and fight. "I'm sad, too. And a little bit mad. But we can't just stay up here. We shouldn't. You have school, and we have church, and we've spent too much time up here missing the good things about our friends down in town. I forgot about those good things for a while, but Miss Dana helped me remember."

"I still don't wanna go. Why do I hafta?"

Mason wasn't sure how far to push this. The old Mason would have given in to retreat. The new Mason wasn't so easily beaten, nor did he want his son to surrender to what had happened. "School is one of those things we have to do. Even when it doesn't feel fun. And are you sure you don't want to go to Special Ladies Day? I mean, you already invited Miss Dana. I think she was looking forward to it."

"Even now? You just said people were mean."

In fact, going to the school event seemed like a good way to push back against the fear and bitterness. "What would you think if I said most especially now?"

"Why?"

Perhaps it was time to celebrate this special lady, because she was still special—very special—no matter what people thought. "Because Miss Dana *is* special. She's just as special today as she was yesterday." *Even more so*, he thought to himself. "I like Miss Dana." *A whole lot*.

"Me, too."

"And those people in town who don't think she's very special right now? On account of the camp? I think they're wrong. Don't you?"

Charlie nodded. "They're a hundred percent wrong."

Mason smiled at the pint-sized endorsement. "She's just as sad about what happened as you and I are. So we need to show everyone how special we know she is. Seems to me you've got a pretty good opportunity to do that. I mean, the whole thing is called Special Ladies Day, right?"

"You can't come," Charlie pointed out. "It's just for special ladies."

"I know. And I would if I could. But that means this is a job only you can do." *Maybe a job only God can do.*

"Everybody will look at me funny. Or her."

Charlie wasn't wrong. "Maybe at first. And only the people who don't really matter to you and me. Our friends already know how special Miss Dana is." How long had it been since he'd thought of the people down in town as his friends? Far too long. And it might have gone on for far longer if not for Dana. "If you go, you and her can show everybody else how special she is." Mason felt he had to add, "But only if you want to. You know I wouldn't make you do it if you really don't want to."

He wasn't going to send a seven-year-old to fight his battles—he was already planning to wage a few of his own—but Charlie's invitation to Dana for Special Ladies Day was starting to look very much like God's hand moving in his life.

Mason was pleased to watch his son come around to the idea. "Can we leave early if we want to?"

"Absolutely. But I think you won't want to. The first little bit might feel squiggly, but not the rest." *Squiggly* was the word he'd come up with to describe the awkward way people treated him and Charlie when Melony first died. They'd stare, or avoid, or say the wrong thing out of the sheer discomfort such a tragedy brought.

Charlie considered his choice. "Okay. But can we get ice cream afterward?"

There was likely to be a whole host of treats at the event, but Mason rather liked a built-in time to spend with Dana afterward. The victory of *we're still here* was worth celebrating, if nothing else. "Sure thing." He gathered up the breakfast dishes. "Go get your stuff together, the bus'll be here soon." There were days Mason almost resented how Bart Salinas poked his nose into Charlie's life. Today, Mason found himself saying a prayer of thanks that someone like Bart was driving the bus and offering all kinds of support to his son. The Busketeers' solid support of Camp True North Springs was an extra treasure right now, and Mason meant to say so as he saw Charlie onto the bus this morning.

As they walked down the drive to wait for the bus, Mason jokingly asked his son, "So should I tell Miss Dana you'll keep your date?"

Charlie rolled his eyes and giggled. "I'm not dating Miss Dana." Then, without so much as a blink of hesitation, he looked at Mason and asked, "Are you?"

How do I answer that? The wonder of their kiss last night seemed to shoot through him all over again. He settled for asking, "Do you think I should?" After all, the answer would tell him a lot about Charlie's readiness to welcome someone new into their lives.

Charlie thought about it for a painfully long time.

For a few minutes, Mason worried the bus might come and collect his son before Charlie gave him an answer. After all, he was still astonished and unsteady about everything that had happened between he and Dana last night. Mason found himself anxious to know what Charlie thought.

"I like her," Charlie declared just as the bus came around the bend. "Do you want me to ask her about it?"

"Oh, no," Mason rushed to answer while still trying to sound as if the whole thing were no big deal. "You can leave that grown-up stuff to us. But if I see her today, I'll remind her about tomorrow." Mason had every intention of making very sure he saw Dana today. They had a lot to talk about.

When the bus came to the head of their driveway, Bart surprised Mason by shutting off the ignition and coming down out of the vehicle once Charlie was on board.

"I just want you to know Rita and I are behind you one hundred percent," he said, shaking Mason's hand. "You're going to fight the denial, aren't you? There's some sort of appeal process? Don't let Arthur win this one. North Springs is better than what you saw last night."

"I know," Mason agreed, feeling it down to his bones for the first time in a long time. "I know. Charlie still wants to bring Dana to Special Ladies Day, and I think he should."

Bart smiled. "I couldn't agree more." He leaned in. "After all, she's one special lady, isn't she?"

Mason returned Bart's knowing look. "That she is."

* * *

"Thanks, Captain, but I'm not interested," Dana said into the phone. She waited for the words to feel like the giant leap they were. They only settled solid and sure in her chest, reminding her that no matter what happened with the commission, running back to Denver would never be the right choice.

"You're sure?" He'd pressed her rather hard during their conversation. It was nice to hear how much he valued her work, how she was missed. Still, the thought of going back—however safe it might appear on the outside—offered no comfort.

"I am." She wasn't that detective anymore. And while Dana still couldn't say who she was becoming, she did like who she'd become so far.

"Well, I guess I'll accept that for now," Captain Derrick replied. "But I'll always find a place for you if you change your mind." He laughed just a little bit, and she could picture him shaking his head, scratching his whiskered chin. "Gotta say, I can't quite picture you out there will all that sand and cactus."

Dana looked out the house window to the park-like setting of the North Springs town square. This far up the mountains, it wasn't all sand and cactus. In fact, there weren't any cacti at all—those flourished at a lower altitude. North Springs had amazing rock formations, tall ponderosa pines, shrubs and lots of plant life. It wasn't lush forest by any stretch, but it wasn't a parched desert, either. All kinds of things—including souls—flourished here. "Thanks for all your support. Tell the precinct Mom said hello."

That last use of her nickname made Derrick laugh loudly. "I'll do that. Take care, Preston. You deserve to be happy."

She sat back as she ended the call, settling into the chair that Mason had repaired. She hadn't burned any bridges with her old colleagues in Denver, but this last phone call felt like a very deliberate exit. An affirmation that her life was going in a new direction.

A text chimed on her phone. Good morning, came the message from Mason.

Hello to you, too, Dana typed back, feeling goofy about the smitten smile on her face.

Breakfast and battle plans?

Those four words said everything Dana wanted to hear. As far as she was concerned Camp True North Springs should not go down without a fight, but she needed to hear it from Mason first. YES, she replied.

Guerro's in 30? Cheeeeeeeeese.

A joke? From Mason Avery on a morning like today? Surely that meant anything was possible. Dana typed back, Yes! and was out the door in twenty minutes.

It probably shouldn't have surprised her to see Hannah and Rita in animated conversation as they walked across the square toward her house. The pair headed straight for her as she turned her key in the latch.

"I can't believe it," Rita said, "I'm fuming. I'm disappointed. I'm a whole lot of things, and none of them good."

"North Springs is better than this," Hannah consoled. "At least I thought North Springs was better than this. How are you? How is Mason?"

Dana was momentarily lost how to answer. Could two people be so good and so awful at the same time? Her life seemed thrown off-balance and falling-into-place at the same time. She expected Mason felt much the same. She settled for replying, "Upset but not surrendered," shrugging her ambivalence to the two women.

"I know exactly how you feel," Hannah agreed, nodding.

Oh, I doubt that, Dana thought. Hannah hadn't just kissed what felt like the love of her life last night. Hannah hadn't just firmly cut ties with her safe past to launch whatever came next. Dana was counting the seconds until she could slip her hands into Mason's and hear him say they'd face whatever came next together.

"So you won't let them win." Rita said it as a declaration of war, not a question. "You'll fight last night's rejection."

"I don't quite know what comes next, Rita."

"Tomorrow is Special Ladies Day," Rita said. "You're still going with Charlie, aren't you? You absolutely should go."

Hannah's eyes brightened. "Charlie invited you to Special Ladies Day at school? How perfect is that! You are a special lady, most especially to him. Oh, Dana, you have to go. Don't you dare let them scare you off of that."

Dana had hoped the same thing. "I will go, if Charlie still wants to. I don't know how Mason broke the news to him this morning. But I guess I'll know soon enough—I'm heading over to Guerro's to meet Mason right now."

"Does Mason sound ready to fight it?" Hannah asked. Given how Mason had secluded himself in past months, it was a fair question.

"He does. I know I am." The question was, would that be enough?

Rita put her hands on her hips, battle ready. "I assure you, we are, too."

"I'm glad to know that," Dana replied. It did mean a lot to her to know Hannah, Rita, Theo and Bart were in her corner.

"Here's what I think," Rita went on. "Last night you saw a bunch of frightened people stirred up by Arthur Nicholson. That's not who we are. Now it's time we showed you the real North Springs. Your camp will happen. Those children, those families, they will find a place of healing up on that mountain." She thumped her chest with one hand, and Dana thought maybe she was far from the only warrior woman in North Springs. "Because I am not going to stop fighting until they do. Arthur thinks the Busketeers are only five men who drive buses. He's wrong. The Busketeers are all of us, and we're about to become a mighty army for good. You just watch."

Dana gave that war cry the only response she could:

she pulled Rita into a fierce hug, and was quickly joined by Hannah. "God bless you, Rita Salinas." She smiled at Hannah. "You, too. I wish Charlie and Mason could hear you both right now."

"I'll be manning the refreshments table tomorrow night in the school gymnasium," Rita said. "I want to see you there. Holding your head up high like the special lady you are. No backing down."

"And if anyone gives you even the slightest hint of trouble, you send them to me," Hannah said. "No one's going to have any reason to doubt you're one of us."

You're one of us. The words wrapped themselves around Dana like a warm welcome. In a remarkably short time this town had adopted her as one of their own, embracing the wild idea she had brought with her. Tears welled up in her eyes as she choked out, "Thank you."

"No thanks needed. Now go on over to breakfast with that man." Rita leaned in. "He's sweet on you. You know that, don't you?" She winked and nudged Hannah, who gave a giggle worthy of a preschooler.

Dana found it was easy not to hide the smile that bubbled up from her heart. If there was a single gesture that signaled healing, it was how she wiped tears away with a smile on her face. *I am home*, her whole body seemed to echo. "Actually, I do."

Rita's eyes popped wide. Hannah grinned. A morning that ought to have felt defeated and dreary seemed to sparkle in the morning sunlight.

"Oooh," Rita nearly squealed, "Arthur Nicholson and his bunch don't stand a chance, now." She waved

Dana in the direction of the diner. "Off with you now. Come by later and tell me all the details."

"And stop by the store *right* after that," Hannah teased, catching Dana's hand with the friendliest of squeezes before walking toward the grocery with a delighted spring in her step.

Dana stopped for just a moment to let the sun's bright rays kiss her face. *Home*, yes. And then she headed for Guerro's diner for breakfast and battle plans with the man who'd captured her heart.

Chapter Eighteen

Charlie gave a lopsided grin as he handed the paper
flower for Dana to pin on like a corsage. He'd given her
name at the check-in desk with the sweetest declaration
of pride. His pronouncement, "This is Miss Dana, my
special lady," had all the grandeur of a valentine, and
Dana was beyond pleased that she'd opted not to miss
the event. When Charlie took her hand to lead her to
his classroom, she felt her throat tighten at the boy's
tender open affection.

However, Dana soon noticed the sideways glance of
one woman in the hallway. Then the outright frown of
another. When another boy and his mother offered an
especially dark look, it didn't surprise Dana that Charlie identified them as Nathan Summers and his mom.

"Are you feeling squiggly, too?" Charlie whispered
as they sat down at his desk to look over a Special Ladies Day card Charlie had waiting there.

"Squiggly?" she asked, finding the odd word rather
fitting.

"That's what Dad calls it when people look at you and make your stomach feel all funny," Charlie explained.

Her stomach did feel as if it had been squiggling since they entered the school. "Yep," she admitted, squeezing Charlie's hand. "What do you do for the squigglies?" She found she very much wanted to hear his answer.

"You tell 'em to go away and do what you want to do."

Good advice. Dana offered Charlie a knowing wink. "Get gone, squigglies," she declared just loud enough for both of them to hear. "I want to have fun with Charlie."

His giggle was the best squiggly antidote anyone could hope for. "Good job." Charlie nodded his approval.

A friendly-looking woman walked up to the desk. "So this is Miss Dana," she said. "Charlie's told me a lot about you." She extended a hand. "I'm Mrs. Booker."

"She's my teacher," Charlie explained.

"And a friend of Mason's, and Mike from the hardware store is my nephew. Your pond idea was wonderful. I've had more than one student wish for a Franco of their own."

Dana wasn't quite sure what to say. So much of what happened with that pond that day felt like it had come from beyond her. Ordained, as she and Mason had begun to say—of so much that was unfolding around them. "I was happy about it all."

"You seem to have a lot of good ideas. I'm sorry everyone doesn't seem to see it that way. As you can imagine, I'm very much in favor of what you and Mason have proposed. I hope you won't let the meeting the other night stop you from making it happen."

"I'm glad to hear that," Dana replied. She hoped she could hear words like that tonight at least as many times as she caught the judgmental looks. That was part of the point of tonight, in addition to spending this important time with Charlie.

Mrs. Booker seemed to realize that as she looked at Charlie. "Charlie, how about we help Miss Dana meet the other special ladies? Tommy and his mom are over there by the book report displays."

Charlie looked up at Dana. "Wanna go meet Tommy? He likes frogs, too."

"Sure thing." Right there was the strategy Dana knew would mount her best defense against Arthur Nicholson and his fearmongering. Meeting other families from North Springs, one at a time. Making friends. Inserting herself into the community she knew she wanted to call home. Ideas were powerful, facts and plans were useful, but relationships were what would bring Camp True North Springs to life. What would bring her own self back to life.

So Dana started by making a new friend at the book report display. And then another at the sing-along in the music room, where she discovered Charlie had no more ability to carry a tune than she did. Still, there was a goofy joy in simply being loud and happy no matter how off-key. She found herself able to compliment Brenda Summers—the woman whose car Charlie had hit with the rock—on her beautiful singing voice despite the sharp glare Brenda gave Dana. The school librarian invited her to a book club even as the vice principal's cold scowl told her Camp True North Springs did not have his approval.

All in all, Dana found herself exhausted and ready for the promise of Rita's friendly face by the time they made it to the refreshment table in the gymnasium. After gathering up drinks and cupcakes from Rita, Charlie and Dana sat down at one of the little decorated tables that were set up all over the large room like a giant festive tea party.

One woman Dana remembered from the art room waved hello from the next table, her arm bearing a brightly colored beaded bracelet just like the one Dana now wore. Charlie and her had made it together, and Dana loved the sight of it on her wrist.

Another woman came up to their table a few minutes later. "Are you the person proposing the camp with Mason?"

"I am," she said, glad to feel confidence in the declaration.

"For what it's worth," she said, "I think it's a good idea. My nephew was killed in combat last year, and my sister's still reeling. We all are. Could they come? When it opens, I mean?"

Dana took a spark of satisfaction that the woman had said *when* rather than *if*. "The camp will be for someone exactly like that. I'm sorry for your loss, and for your sister's."

The woman put her hands on her son's shoulders. "Sounds like it would end up being a pretty special place. I know some folks are against it, but…well, you have my support. I'm Lisa. I'm not on the committee or anything, but I wanted you to know I think it should go through."

She offered Lisa a smile. "Thank you. That means a lot. I hope there are a lot more people who feel the way you do."

"You know," she replied with a look around the room, "I think there are. Don't give up, okay?"

That exchange warmed Dana's heart, until another woman and her daughter went to sit at a nearby table. Once the woman saw Dana, she threw a "what on earth are you doing here?" glower at her and moved on to a different table. *You win some, you lose some*, Dana thought, still finding tonight mostly on the win side.

Rita gave the frowning woman a loud cluck of disapproval as she made her way to the table. "Some people didn't take their nice pills this morning," she said as she sat down with Dana and Charlie. She wiped the disapproving look off her face and turned to Charlie. "Did you have fun with your special lady?"

"We made a bracelet," Charlie boasted, pointing to Dana's new accessory.

"Well, that's the nicest one I've seen tonight. Special indeed."

"I've been talking you two up all evening. Bart, too. I think we brought a few more folks around to the camp idea. How many more days until the appeal hearing?"

"Five. Arthur didn't waste any time setting it for Wednesday. He wants this over fast, I can tell."

"But Dad says you're gonna ask again," Charlie said, his tongue turning blue from licking the frosting on his cupcake.

"We are," Dana said. The confidence in her voice surprised her.

"And this time, you'll get the answer you're hoping for. With Busketeers and prayer warriors and all kinds of folks getting on board, I don't see how you can lose now."

I can, Dana admitted silently. Some opponents just had too much power over even the worthiest of causes. Still, most of her heart—and now, she could even say her soul—stood ready to believe that God could make a way for this camp if it was in His plan for her life. Even if they only had until Wednesday to make their appeal.

"We made new friends," Charlie said. "I'm glad we came."

"Me, too," Dana could say with total honesty. "I'm really glad you invited me."

Charlie took an enormous bite of his cupcake. "We still get to meet Dad for ice cream after this, right?"

"Who has room for ice cream after all these cupcakes?" Rita teased.

"Me!" Charlie declared.

Ice cream might be nice, but what Dana wanted most of all right now was to be with Mason. *I've fallen for him, hard*, she admitted to herself. That was the sweetest thought of all.

Charlie dug his spoon into the enormous chocolate sundae Mason had bought the three of them to share. He could have bought one twice the size for all the pride he was feeling tonight. Dana had faced both friends and foes at Special Ladies Day, and reports from Rita,

Hannah, and even Martha Booker stated that she had won many people over to the cause of Camp True North Springs.

"I had fun. Did you?" Charlie asked as he dug his spoon into the dish.

Dana caught Mason's eye. He had no doubt Dana had met with a mixed reception. He hoped there had been more shows of support than the challenging remarks and sideways glances.

"It was special," Dana offered. "Squiggly, but special."

Mason laughed. "So you learned about our special word, did you?" That said a lot about the evening.

"Charlie clued me in," she explained.

"Miss Dana and I showed 'em, didn't we?" Charlie said, chocolate-smudged chin raised in defiance. "Squiggly can't stop an Avery, no sir."

"Me, neither," Dana replied, dipping her own spoon in for a sizable helping. "Charlie taught me how to tell those squiggles to get lost. Pretty good practice, I'd say."

Charlie got a look on his face Mason had come to recognize as an "I'm not sure it's okay to ask this" expression. "Whatcha thinking?" he asked his son.

"Jake asked me if Mr. Nicholson hated us. Is Mr. Nicholson a mean man?"

Now there was a huge question from a small boy. Dana looked a little lost for a good answer as well. Mason had swallowed a barrel full of unkind thoughts toward the judgmental man, but that didn't make it okay to admit it to Charlie. Or to let words like hate come into the picture. He cleared his throat. "Mr. Nicholson and I have a big disagreement about the camp. Very big. And, yes, I wish he were nicer about it. But he doesn't hate us, and I don't hate him. I'm trying my best to see that he just feels very strongly. And I think he's a little scared."

"Well, I'm not," Charlie countered with a heartwarming confidence. "I think the camp'll be great."

"That's the way to look at it," Dana finally chimed in. "We're not scared, so that helps other people see they don't have to be scared or mean, either. And tonight was a great start, Charlie. You did an amazing job and I had a terrific time."

Mason knew that wasn't exactly true. Dana had told him she'd worked hard to slough off the handful of dark looks and jabbing comments. It had been a true act of bravery to show up tonight. She'd shown all of North Springs that she—that all of them—had no intention of backing down no matter what kind of a fight Arthur Nicholson put up. Admiration mixed with the attraction and deep affection he'd come to feel for this woman. He could admit it to himself now—this was the beginnings of love. A deep love he thought would never bless his life again. *Thank You, Lord. No matter what happens from here, You've restored so much.* He'd have to find the right moment to tell Dana, but something in her eyes told him she already knew.

"So what do we do now?" Charlie asked.

"Well," Dana replied, "We have an appointment with Mr. Anderson on Monday to draw up the appeal."

"What's that mean?" Charlie asked.

"It means we ask again for permission for the camp to happen," Mason explained.

"With a lot more friends helping us this time," Dana added.

Charlie looked up at him with hopeful eyes. "Will it work?"

"I don't know," Mason answered. "But I think we'll be okay no matter what."

"'Cause of Miss Dana, huh?" Charlie asked the question as if everyone knew the obvious answer.

Dana felt her face flush even as Mason reached under the table to clasp her hand. He already did know, but a wonder of that sort was still worth declaring. "Sorta," Mason said, smirking. More would definitely come, but that was declaration enough for now. "What do you think?" he asked Charlie. "Will we be okay no matter what 'cause of Miss Dana?"

Charlie nodded, and Mason felt the true healing of his family take hold. He wanted to make Camp True North Springs happen—badly—but he also knew that his long exile from life had come to an end. If Dana had come to North Springs to set something right, she'd done far more than that. She'd brought his heart back to life.

Chapter Nineteen

"**O**rder!" Arthur Nicholson banged his gavel to hush the low roar of conversation that filled the town hall meeting room Wednesday evening. "I will remind all of you that while commentary is accepted, the final decision on this appeal rests with the zoning committee alone." He had the tone of a general commanding his troops to hold the line.

Dana looked around the room. Every seat was filled. She tried to read the faces of the crowd to see if there were more people here to support the camp or to ensure that the variance was again denied. She found she couldn't hope to say, and that gave her gut a solid case of the squigglies that refused to subside.

Dana clutched the small rock Charlie had lent to her again tonight. If there was ever a moment where she needed perspective, this was it. So much had gone beyond her dreams here in North Springs, but so much felt as if it hung on the outcome of tonight. Was that true? Was she ready to accept whatever happened in this room tonight? *Not yet*, she told herself. *I'm still ready to fight for this.*

For them, she added as she felt Mason give her hand a quick squeeze under the table where they sat ready to present their appeal. For Charlie and Mason, and for all the victims to follow behind them in what Camp True North Springs could be. Dana prayed that the vision she—and Mason and Charlie and Theo and Hannah and all the Busketeers, for that matter—had sparked among these people took hold. There was so much good that could be done. So much healing to be had. So much hope to give.

Dana twisted to look over her shoulder to where Charlie sat between Rita and Bart, and sent the boy a playful "we got this" wink. Charlie had insisted on coming. She and Mason had talked it over, and decided it would be okay. If they did receive a victory tonight, it seemed important that Charlie be there to witness it.

"But if they're going to deny it, I want them to have to do it to Charlie's face," Mason had said. "And a child in the audience might help people watch their tongues, which I wouldn't mind."

Protect him, Dana prayed for the boy she'd come to love. Rita and Bart had promised to whisk Charlie out of the room if things got ugly, but for now his sweet presence lent her strength and courage. She and Mason would give tonight everything they had.

But, ultimately, it was all in God's hands, wasn't it? They could present all the facts and statistics and persuasion in the world, and it would still be God that softened the hearts of the seven people in front of her.

"Mason, you may begin." Arthur's voice was dripping with condescension.

Mason rose with a calm clarity. "My father always told me land had a purpose," he began. "That we, as its owners, were really more like caretakers, allowing the land to fulfill that purpose. To grow things, to sustain life, to shelter or even just to add beauty. It was always bigger than just the Avery family."

He stepped out from behind the table. "I confess that since Melony's death I haven't done a good job of that caretaking. I let the huge loss almost bury me alongside my wife." His voice broke a bit on that confession, and Dana felt her throat tighten. He went on. "And I'm grateful to all of you who tried to reach out and be friends and neighbors to Charlie and me. It's what I've always loved about North Springs. What's always made it home."

"It *is* your home," Rita called out. "Always will be." Her show of support earned a reprimanding glare from Arthur, but Dana was glad to hear a few supportive murmurs echo Rita's words.

"Now I believe I know the purpose of my land. I'll admit, I didn't take much to Dana's idea at first," Mason continued. "But she can be a persistent lady, and she could see what I couldn't. Camp True North Springs needs to happen. The land needs it. There are families who need it. Our world needs it." He paused for a moment, regaining his composure before saying, "*I* need it."

"Maybe *we* don't," came one sharp call from somewhere in the back of the room. Dana turned to see the mother who'd moved to another table at Special Ladies Day. "No one needs that sort here."

Nicco stood up. "That sort, Carol, is me." Arthur banged his gavel, but Nicco just glared right back and kept on speaking. "That sort is way more people than you realize. Sure, some folks bring trouble down on themselves, but a lot more just have it show up on their doorstep. Could be you tomorrow. Could be any of us. I want to know there's a place like this for them to come heal. I wasted way too many years on account of not having any place like it." Nicco looked around the room. "It's grace and mercy, people. How on earth can you be against grace and mercy?"

"We have every right to fear this," one of the town's real estate brokers said. "Home values'll drop for sure."

Another man stood up, asking, "Did the rehab center do that?" Dana recognized him as Sebastian Costa, who'd gently inquired the other day if they thought the camp might need a cook when it opened. Arthur banged his gavel again but just like Nicco, Sebastian paid no mind. Dana didn't know whether to be glad or worried that Arthur seemed to have lost control of the room.

"That center brought me to this town," Sebastian went on. "I bought a condo here when I chose to stay. You sold me that place, Mark. Nothing's harmed all your precious property values."

"They might not all be like you, Seb," Mark replied.

"And what is like me, Mark? Are you really ready to say you're that much different than me? Or any of your kids? Or that anyone doesn't deserve some of the chances you've had?"

Hannah stood up. "Come on, people, we're better than this. We've got a chance to do something amazing here. And we don't even have to do it. We just have to allow Mason and Dana to do it. Although you can be sure I'll help in any way I can. I don't know if this is who we are, but I'm pretty sure this is who we *ought* to be."

The meeting went on for another hour, with commentary flying back and forth between North Springs residents in favor of, and opposed to, the needed variance. Dana and Theo mostly let Mason speak, although each of them offered some details or logistical specifics when one of the committee members had a question.

Only it was never really an issue of those kinds of practicalities. Tonight was a moral—or more accurately, a spiritual—battle for the soul of what North Springs was going to be. Whether fear and worry would win, or whether hope and grace would prevail.

"We're long past the allotted time for public comment," Arthur finally said. "I move that we call the vote."

Mason reached for Dana's hand. She clasped his strong hand in hers, suddenly realizing they were both holding Charlie's rock together. It was a tiny, affirming detail that reminded her what she'd gained here in North Springs went far beyond whatever vote came down tonight.

Slowly—with more drama than was necessary, Dana thought—the town clerk called for each committee member's vote.

The North Springs Planning and Zoning Committee approved the variance five to two. Only Arthur and Paul Summers remained opposed.

Charlie's resulting whoop of joy pretty much said it all.

The world had shifted. Mason had the sure sense that each hour took him up out of the valley and toward his new life. The good night kiss he'd given Dana last night—in front of Charlie no less, so that took a bit of explaining—was as sweet as any kiss he'd ever known. Bart's victory honk at the bus stop this morning was crazy joyful, as bright and hopeful as the look Charlie had worn on his face since the winning vote. It had been a good choice to let Charlie come. His son was getting a front row seat to the new possibilities in their lives, and that was a gift.

So was the woman whose oddball doorbell he rang this morning, newspaper in hand.

"Hi," she said when she opened the door. She was so beautiful. How had he not seen that from the first moment he'd laid eyes on her just beyond his gate?

Mason kissed her again, just because it was such a wonder to do so. "I love you," he said as he brushed her cheek.

She made the most adorable sound, something between a hum and a purr. A happy sound. "So you said last night. Several times."

He grinned, feeling like he could shout a whoop just like Charlie's. "You did, too."

"I did." Her green eyes glowed. "I do."

He held up the paper. "We did it." He had folded it

open to a specific page. "I think I'm going to have this framed."

Dana took the paper from him and read aloud the words he'd been savoring all morning:

The North Springs Messenger Midweek Edition
Minutes of the North Springs AZ Zoning Commission Special Meeting
Called to order at 7:00 p.m.

Agenda: reconsideration of zoning variance 18-A for the parcel of land currently owned by Mason Avery from residential to commercial use.

After lengthy testimony from multiple residents and further documentation submitted, a second vote was taken.

The variance request passed with five votes in favor, two votes against.

The meeting adjourned at 8:50 p.m.

Renovations to create Camp True North Springs on the Avery property are expected to begin soon with an initial trial session to launch over the summer.

"Soon," she said. "I like the sound of that."

"Me, too," Mason said. "What do you say we go over to Guerro's and make plans?"

Dana's smile widened. "I like the sound of that even more."

Epilogue

Two months later

Dana tucked in the corner of the last blanket on the last bunk bed. Every blanket—and most of the towels and other linens at the camp—were blue. It was a brave color. A color of courage and protection. The color of water, of springs nourishing the dry land. If true north had a color, Dana was sure it was blue.

"We're ready." It felt so amazing to declare that.

"How long 'til they get here?" Charlie asked. Charlie had asked that question hourly today. And much of yesterday.

Mason finished writing a name on the small chalkboard that sat on each bedroom door. "Just before dinner. Same as the last time you asked. Find a little bit more patience there, kiddo."

Charlie bounced on the bed Dana had just made. "I just want to meet them. Now. I bet they're nice. What's Chef Seb making them for dinner, anyways?"

"Tacos," she replied, shooing him off with a laugh as she bent to smooth the blankets again. "Same as the last time you asked." Sebastian Costa was the first official employee of Camp True North Springs, coming on board for this trial run of three families for a June weekend now that school was out. It was finally happening. The glow of hope and satisfaction in her heart rivaled the strongest Arizona sunshine. "With lots of cheese."

"'Cause you looove cheese," Charlie teased, wiggling his fingers.

"Yes, I do." Dana ruffled the boy's hair, feeling a surge of love for him. "Are you sure you're ready to make some new friends?"

"Yep! I am. All of 'em. Even the ones that aren't so nice at first." Dana had tried to help Charlie understand that some of their guests had heavy hearts and carried big burdens. It amazed her how much grace Charlie's tiny heart could extend to people he hadn't even met yet. Right there was the wonder of Camp True North Springs playing out in front of her.

"What's Chef Seb making for dessert?" Charlie asked, clearly more concerned with practical details like food.

"Why don't you go ask him?" Mason suggested. With that, Charlie took off in the direction of the house kitchen.

Dana laughed. "You know Seb said he's making churros for dessert."

Mason tugged on her hand until he pulled her into an embrace. She cherished his hands. They were strong and sure and gifted. So much of him showed up in the woodwork and design of all the camp's buildings. He'd built each of the bunks and beds himself, and had refinished the most beautiful desk for her office in the main house. So much had changed for him, in him, since that fateful day she arrived at his gate.

"I know," he said to her remark. "But I wanted a moment to tell you how much I love you. Again. Before all the chaos starts."

"I love you, too," she replied, enjoying how wonderful a wide grin felt on her face. The words left her lips so easily these days. How amazing was that? "But it won't be chaos. You know me, I planned everything down to the last detail."

"Oh, I'm sure you have it all planned out. But that doesn't mean there can't be a few surprises."

"You know I'm not a big fan of surprises," she teased. Her smile turned to astonishment as Mason reached into his back pocket and produced a small black box.

"But this one is a very good surprise." Mason got down on one knee, and Dana's heart fluttered as he opened the box to reveal an exquisite ring.

Surrounded as they were by breathtaking scenery, there still could be no other place for Mason to get down on one knee than here in the old barn that now housed rooms for parents and children. Rooms built by her plans, Mason's craftsmanship and a small army of enthusiastic contractors. Rooms built faster than she imagined by God's purpose and the grace of a whole community. Dana's sense of wonder at all of it nearly knocked her off her feet.

"I think it's time to take our partnership to a new level," Mason said with the warmest of smiles. "Charlie, too."

Dana's hands were shaking. "He knows?"

"You don't think all that excitement is over just the first guests, do you?" Mason slid the ring onto her finger, where it sparkled with perfection and promise. "Marry me?"

"Yes!" Dana exclaimed. "Of course I will. I want nothing more than to be a family with you and Charlie."

"You already are our family." Mason rose to kiss her with all the tenderness she'd come to love about this man. "You are our true north. You were from the beginning. It just took me a while to figure it out."

Dana slipped her arms around Mason's neck and felt the world fall into perfect place. "It was all worth waiting for."

"Dad!" Charlie's voice was heard behind them. "Stop getting mushy with Dana. Someone's coming up the drive already."

"This early?" Mason winced. "I'd hoped for a little more time to celebrate."

"I guess the surprises are starting now," Dana replied. "Let's go meet them."

They walked out of the old barn, hand in hand.

* * * * *

Dear Reader,

Welcome to North Springs! I'm delighted you are starting this series with Dana, Mason and dear little Charlie. Camp True North Springs will see new stories of faith and love as more families come "up the mountain" to heal and find new hope. Dana and Mason show us that places which look like dry and barren endings can become flourishing new beginnings under God's hand.

Join me for the next book in the series where camp staff cook Seb Costa learns that the fresh starts in life don't just happen to True North Springs campers—God changes the lives of everyone who opens their heart to His purpose.

I'd love it if you connected with me at alliepleiter.com, on Instagram, and Facebook. If good old postal mail is your thing, you can also reach me at PO Box 7026, Villa Park, IL 60181.

Blessings to you and yours,
Allie

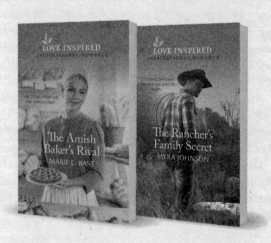